1 MONTH OF
FREE
READING

at

www.ForgottenBooks.com

By purchasing this book you are eligible for one month membership to ForgottenBooks.com, giving you unlimited access to our entire collection of over 1,000,000 titles via our web site and mobile apps.

To claim your free month visit:

www.forgottenbooks.com/free11658

ISBN 978-0-483-74181-2
PIBN 10011658

This book is a reproduction of an important historical work. Forgotten Books uses
state-of-the-art technology to digitally reconstruct the work, preserving the original format
whilst repairing imperfections present in the aged copy. In rare cases, an imperfection in
the original, such as a blemish or missing page, may be replicated in our edition. We do,
however, repair the vast majority of imperfections successfully; any imperfections that
remain are intentionally left to preserve the state of such historical works.

THE

NURSERY

A MAGAZINE

For Youngest Readers.

BY

Fanny P. Seaverns.

VOLUME I.

BOSTON:
JOHN L. SHOREY, No. 13, WASHINGTON STREET.
1867.

Electrotyped and Printed by GEO. C. RAND & AVERY, Boston.

THE NURSERY.

HOW THE CAT WAS GOOD TO THE BIRD.

"I CAN tell you a strange tale of a cat."

"Oh, do tell it! Is it a true tale?"

"Yes: it is a true tale. A friend of mine had a pet cat and a tame bird; and the name of the cat was Fun; and

Fun was so fond of the bird, that it would play with it for an hour at a time.

"Was it not queer to see a cat and a bird at play? The bird would hop out of its cage, and fly down to the cat; and the cat would put out its paw, and give the bird a soft pat on its head, as much as to say, 'How do you do, this fine day? I am so glad to see you!'

"And then the bird would sit, and sing to the cat a song; and the cat would cry, 'Mew, mew, mew,' as if it would like to say, 'Thank you; that was a nice song; I did like that nice song.' And then the bird would fly a short way off, and the cat would run to try and catch it; and then the bird would fly off once more, and the cat would run and jump, and do all that it could to get up to the side of the bird; and then the two would have such a game of play!

"One day, when these two were at high romps, all at once the cat made a great spring, took hold of the bird by its neck, and ran with it out of the room."

"Oh! did it harm the poor little bird?"

"You shall hear. It was all done in so short a time, that my friend could not stop the cat; but, as you may well think, it gave my friend much pain to think that the cat should rush on the bird in that way, and take it in its mouth by the neck, as if to kill it.

"As quick as she could, my friend got up from her chair to go and see what the cat had done with the bird. But just then, what should she spy but an old strange cat, that lay hid like a thief at one end of the room.

"'Oh, dear!' thought my friend; 'what can this old strange cat want here? Why, it must have come to try to catch and eat my poor little bird. And my good cat, Fun, took the little bird off to save it from the claws of this great strange cat.'

"So my friend drove the great strange cat from the room as fast as she could; and then my friend went to the door, and called, 'Fun, Fun, Fun! come here, Fun!'

"And by and by, what should she hear but, 'Chirp, chirp, chirp; chirp, chirp, chirp: and then, Mew, mew, mew; mew, mew, mew.'

"And then in came the bird, hop, hop, hop; hop, hop, hop: and the good cat Fun came close by its side, — so close! And the cat looked now this way and now that, as much as to say, 'Is that old strange cat quite gone? If not, it is not safe for my dear bird to be here.'

"And when Fun saw that the old strange cat was quite gone, oh! it was so glad, — so glad! And it put its soft paw on the bird, and gave it a pat, as much as to say, 'There, now you are safe, — quite safe! That great strange cat is gone, — quite gone. Now we may play and romp once more.'

"And the bird sang out a glad song; oh! such a glad song of joy, that it seemed to say, as plain as words, 'My good cat, my nice cat, my kind cat, my brave Fun, oh, how I do thank you for what you have done for me! How I do love you! how I do thank you, my dear, nice, kind, good, brave cat.'"

If a cat and a bird could so learn to a-gree,
How kind to all creat'ures should *we* learn to be!
Now a Hap'py New Year to the cat and the bird,
And to all the good folks who our sto'ry have heard!
Next month to our NURSERY come, you shall find
New sto'ries, new pict'ures, more food for the mind.

HOW JACK FROST COULD NOT CATCH THE LITTLE BOY.

JACK FROST.

WHO are you, lit'tle boy, on your way to the mead'ow,
This cold win'ter day, with your skates and your sled-O?

LITTLE BOY.

My name is Tom Rud'dy; and, though it is snow'ing,
To the mead'ow, to skate and to coast, I am go'ing.

JACK FROST.

You had bet'ter turn back now, my lit'tle friend Tom'my;
For the ground it is stiff, and the day it is storm'y.

LITTLE BOY.

No, sir, if you please, I do love this cold weath'er;
And my coat is of wool, and my shoes are of leath'er.

JACK FROST.

To nip you, and pinch you, and chill you, I'll stud'y,
Un-less you turn back, and run home, Thom'as Rud'dy.

LITTLE BOY.

And who may you be, sir, to talk to me thus, sir?
And what have I done, you should make such a fuss, sir?

JACK FROST.

My name and my call'ing, I will not dis-sem'ble ;
JACK FROST is my name, Tom !   Hear that, Tom, and
  trem'ble !

LITTLE BOY.

Oh! you are the Frost, then, whose touch is so bit'ter ;
Who made all our win'dow-panes spar'kle and glit'ter !

JACK FROST.

Yes, I am that Frost ; and now, Tom, I am com'ing,
To nip you, and pinch you, your fin'ger-tips numb'ing.

LITTLE BOY.

My fin'gers lie snug in my gay lit'tle mit'tens ;
And the fur of my cap is as warm as a kit'ten's.

JACK FROST.

I will breathe on your ears till they tin'gle, — so, fear me,
And scam'per, Tom, scam'per ! — Boo-hoo !   Do you hear
  me ?

LITTLE BOY.

I hear you — I know you — and, if you can match me
In run'ning and sli'ding, come, catch me, Frost ! catch me !

JACK FROST.

Stop ! stop ! — He is gone, all my ter'rors de-fy'ing ;
To scare boys like Tom, I may well give up tr....g.

EMILY CARTER.

THE DOVE AND THE BEE.

On a hot day in June, a dove sat on the branch of a tree that bent down to the brink of a small lake. And the dove saw a poor bee in the lake; saw that the bee would drown if no one could help it.

The dove was good and kind; so what did the dove do but pull off, with its beak, a leaf from the tree, and drop it in the lake, so that the bee could reach the leaf, and climb on to it with its wee legs.

The wind then blew the leaf with the bee on it, all wet, to the shore. The bee did dry its wings in the sun, and look up at the dove, and buzz, as if it would like to say, if it could but speak, "You are a dear, kind dove; and I hope I shall live to do you a good turn."

The bee soon had her wish. As she rose to trim her wings, and to look round, she saw a man with a gun take aim at the dear, kind dove, to shoot her. "Oh, that must not be! that shall not be!" thought the bee. "That man shall not kill my dear, kind friend, the dove, who did drop a leaf to me, and did save my life. I will sting that man before he can fire the gun."

So the bee flew at the face of the man, and stung him on the cheek with so sharp a sting, that the man did cry out

with pain, and did drop his gun as if he had been sh
Bang went the gun as it fell; but the aim was not rig
and the shot from the gun did not hit the dear, kind dove.

Are you not glad the dove was not shot? You thus s
that kind deeds do breed kind deeds. The dove was go
to the bee, and then the bee was good to the dove. T
dove flew off to her nest; and her young ones did coo a
stretch their bills, so full of joy were they to see her. B
the dove did not know what the bee had done.

So you see, if we do good, good will come to us, thou
we may not know how or from whom it may come, or th
good has come at all. We can-not do good to oth'ers wi
out do'ing good at the same time, in some way, to our-selv
And we can-not do harm to oth'ers with-out do'ing harm
the same time, in some way, to our-selves.

Once I knew a bad boy who did pelt an old man in t
street with snow-balls. The old man told him to stop; b
the bad boy kept on, and at last hit the old man in the e
with a lump of ice, and then ran off. The old man w
much hurt.

The bad boy thought no more of it. A year went l
and one day an old man came to his house to lend mon'
to the bad boy's fa'ther, who would fail if he could not {
help. When the old man saw the bad boy, the old m
said to the fa'ther, " I shall lend you no mon'ey; for, if y
can not bring up your son to treat old folks well, you ε
not fit to be trust'ed." Then the old man left the hou
Thus did the bad boy bring ru'in on his own fa'ther. Th
did his sin find him out.

LY CARI

INFANT'S SONG.

(To a Scotch Air.)

WE are but little children
    yet;
We are but little children
    yet!
But, as we grow, the more
    we know :
We hope we may be wiser
    yet.
We wish to learn to read
    and spell ;
We wish to know our duty well !
And every one who asks we'll tell
That we shall soon be wiser yet.

Perhaps we are but naughty yet ;
Perhaps we are but naughty yet !
But every day we try to say,
We'll be a little better yet.
We mean to mind what we are told ;
And, if we should be rude or bold,
We'll try to mend as we grow old :
We'll wish that we were better yet !

You think we are too giddy yet ;
You think we are too giddy yet !
But wait a-while, you need not smile,
Perhaps you'll see us steady yet.
For though we love to run and play,
And many a foolish word we say,
Just come again on some fine day,
You'll find us all quite steady yet !

"JUST FOUR YEARS OLD."

AM four years old to-day, and my name is Mary May-
. I have not been to
l yet; but I know the
s of all the let′ters, and
read short words.

IY aunt gave me a wax
  She gave it to me last
Year's Day. It had red
s and blue eyes, and
 a hat made of green

ou can-not guess the
 of my doll. Well, you
 not try. Her name
lice Pet. I gave that
 to her. She had red
 and blue socks, and a
un-shade made of white
  She had brown curls
r head, and a blue silk
ound her waist.
ne day Dick came home
  Do you want to know
Dick is? Dick is my
er. He did not like

Álice Pet. He had a spite a-gainst Alice Pet. One day he told me he did hate the sight of her. He said she turned in her toes, and had a snub nose. She could not help that — could she? That was no fault of hers — was it? Dick said he had a cure for her snub nose, that would set it all right, and make a beau'ty of her.

"What do you think Dick did? He took my poor Alice Pet, and held her to the fire, and, as her nose was made of wax, it soon be-gan to melt; and then Dick did press it with his thumb till he made the nose quite flat, and so did spoil my poor doll's good looks. Then he did laugh at Alice Pet, and make a low bow to her, and mock her. Was not Dick a bad boy?

"But I did not cry. My moth'er came in; and, when she saw what Dick had done, she did not like it at all. She said to Dick, 'I bought you a new sled to-day, sir, which I had meant to give you; but now I shall give it to Arthur.'

"When Dick found he could not have the sled, he be-gan to cry. My moth'er said to me, 'What shall I do, Mary?' And I said, 'Let us for-give him this time, moth'er.' But moth'er said, 'No; he has been a bad boy, and he must not be let off.'

"So Dick lost his sled, be-cause he was so bad to Alice Pet. But my aunt gave me a new doll, twice as large as the one Dick spoiled. You may hold the nose of my new doll to the fire, and it will not melt. I love my new doll, but I shall not for-get my dear Alice Pet.

"Dick says I am too old to play with dolls. He says I shall be five years old next De-cem'ber; which is true. But Dick is eight years old, and he plays with a tin gun. Do you not think that is as bad as play'ing with a doll? Say. If you will come to my house, you shall hold my doll, and dress it."

Christmas Hymn

HARK! what bells of joy we hear
On this day to children dear!
All the ground with snow is white:
Let our hearts be pure and light!
    Jesus Christ was born this day;
    He to heaven doth lead the way:
    Let us try to do his will,
    And his law of love fulfil.

Let us for the poor have care;
Let us from our plenty spare:
Help the little children who
Have, to help and teach them, few!
    Jesus Christ was born this day;
    He to heaven doth lead the way:
    Let us try to do his will,
    And his law of love fulfil.

"Suffer them to come to me!
Little children, come!" said he;
We his holy word will heed,
For his help from sin we need.
    Jesus Christ was born this day;
    He to heaven doth lead the way:
    Let us try to do his will,
    And his law of love fulfil.

ANNA LIVINGSTON.

11

A GREAT ST. BERNARD DOG.

How do you do, you fine old dog?
The old dog can not say, How do you do?
But the old dog can say, Bow-wow-wow!
The old dog can run and leap and play;
The old dog did save the life of a boy;
The boy came near to die on the ice:
The dog did lift him up from the ice;
And then the dog did bark loud for aid, —
H● ●d bark till men ran to aid the boy.
This fine old dog will not hurt the cat:
You can see him at play with the cat.

HOW BOB WAS A GOOD DOG, AND TIT WAS A BAD DOG.

"I can tell you an odd tale of two dogs; and, as it is a true tale, I think you will like it."

"Do tell it; for I like to hear tales that are true."

"A friend of mine had two dogs. The one was a wee, wee dog, — oh, so wee! but the oth'er was not so small. These two dogs were great friends, though, as you will learn, they were as un-like as they could be.

"Bob was a kind, good dog, who did not wish to bark nor snap nor bite. Here is a pict'ure of Bob. Does he not look like a nice, good dog? But Tit was not a good dog. He liked to bark and snap and bite, and thought that a fight was good fun; that is to say, when he was not in the fight, and when his friend Bob would fight for him, for Tit did not like at all to fight for him-self.

BOB, THE GOOD DOG.

"So if Tit went out for a walk with his mas'ter, and Bob was not with him, Tit would keep quite close to his mas'ter, and would not so much as

13

bark at a dog; but if Bob went out for a walk at the same time — ah! who was so bold a dog as Tit was then?

"As soon as he saw a big dog come his way, Tit would run up to him as fast as his small legs could move, and then would jump up at the big dog's nose, and bark and bark and bark, and do all he could to put the big dog in a rage.

"Some-times the big dog would care no more for Tit than if he had been a fly who came to buzz round his face, and would just give him a pat with his great paw, and put him on one side, as much as to say, 'What a sil'ly lit'tle thing you are to make such a noise, and try and put me in a rage! Do you think I shall put my-self in a rage with such a wee thing as you? If you are a fool, you may be sure I am not one.'

"And then all that was left for Tit to do was to run back to Bob, and make out the best case for himself that he could.

"But some-times when Tit went on in this way to tease a big dog, the big dog would turn round on him, and give a great growl; and Tit thought this fine fun, and he would bark and snap the more, till he had put the big dog in such a rage, that he would take Tit up by the neck, and give him a shake.

"But Tit did not think that this part of it was fine fun at all. So he would call out with a sad, sad cry, as much as to say, 'Bob, Bob, Bob! come here! come quick! Oh, do come, Bob! Make haste! I am hurt! I am hurt! See what this big dog is do'ing!'

"And when Bob heard the cry, off he would run, as hard as he could run: no one could stay or stop him; and he would fly at the big dog who had hold of Tit. Bob did not mind how big the dog was; for Bob was such a kind, brave, good dog, he did not once think of him-self, or how much he might be hurt. Bob thought but of how he could best help his friend.

"But when the big dog did let go his hold, and did turn round to fight Bob, then Tit would not wait to see how the fight would go ; but he would run off fast, — just as fast as he could, — and would not stay nor stop till he got to some safe place, where he could see the fight out at his ease, and feel sure that the big dog would not come near to touch him.

"And then, when Tit felt that he was quite safe, this bad lit'tle dog would bark out, as much as to say, 'Fight him, Bob ; fight him, Bob ! Give it to him well ! Good Bob ! Brave Bob ! That's a fine dog ! Fight him — fight him, Bob !'"

TIT, THE BAD DOG.

"Oh, what a lit'tle cow'ard Tit was !'"

"Yes ; for he would not so much as stay by his friend, to see if his friend was hurt or not. And so poor Bob would have to fight the fight out all by him-self, and would come back torn and hurt, all for the sake of this bad dog of whom he was so fond."

"Oh, that was too bad ! was it not ?"

"Yes, it was too bad ; and in the end Tit had to pay dear for his fun : for when the mas'ter of the two dogs found that if Tit went out for a walk with Bob there was sure to be a fight, but if Bob went out by him-self then Bob was as good as a dog could be, then the mas'ter made up his mind that Tit should not go out for a walk at all.

"And so, when the mas'ter went out for a nice long walk, he would shut Tit up in a room by himself, and take Bob out for the nice long walk. So Tit had to stay by him-self, and think what a bad dog he had been, whilst Bob was out in the fresh air, as full of fun and play as a good dog could be."

BEGINNING TO WALK.

Ring the great bell in the steeple!
Beat the drum, call all the people:
   Baby has begun to walk!

Steady, darling! Steady, steady!
Mother's arms, you see, are ready:
   Do not be afraid to walk!

Come, all folks, come here, and gay be!
Come and see our darling baby:
   Baby has begun to walk!

Emily Carter.

16

THE ALPHABET OF ALPHABETS.

A B . C D

A Arthur and Albert are eating apples.

B Benjamin is busy with the butterflies.

C Clara comes with cherries.

D Dora dances her doll. Dina holds hers.

For a continuation of this Alphabet, see page 49.

17

WINTER AND THE CHILDREN.

Old Winter, in his coat so white,
Is knocking at the door to-night.

CHILDREN.

"Ah, Mr. Winter! is that you?
Glad are we to see you, — how do you do?
We thought you a long way off, you know,
Yet here you are all covered with snow;
And, since you are come, you may just tell us all
What you have brought for us children small."

WINTER.

"Oh! I have brought you more than you can take, —
A Christmas merry, with pies, fruit, and cake;
A plenty of nice, smooth, slippery ice,
Where you can catch a tumble in a trice.
Now you may slide, and make snow-balls beside,
And on your sleds have many a ride;
Make a snow-house and a snow-man too:
Such are the gifts that Winter brings to you."

18

HOW THE DONKEY PUT A STOP TO THE NOISE OF THE PIGS.

. "A FRIEND of mine had a pet don'key, who had a field all to him-self, where he could walk or run, or lie down, or eat or sleep, and, in fact, do as he liked. So in time he came to think the field was all his own, and that no one had the right to come and share his field with him.

19

"But one day two pigs were put in the field. And, when the don'key saw them come in, he looked up at them, as much as to say, 'Hul-lo! Who are you, I should like to know; and what do you want here?' But as he was a kind, good don'key, he did not go near the pigs to drive them off, or to do them harm. He on'ly gave a loud bray, as much as to say, 'The field is wide, and there is room for all three of us; but you must keep the peace, and not fight and squeal.'

"And then munch, munch, munch, the don'key went on eat'ing his grass. But by and by he heard a squeak, — oh, such a loud squeak! And he looked up, and saw the two pigs fight'ing for some fruit which had been put in the field.

"Now, if these pigs had been wise, good pigs, they would have eat'en their fruit in peace, for there was more fruit than they could eat; but, as soon as one pig saw the oth'er take a bit, he would run and push and shove, and try to get the bit from him, and squeal, as if he meant to say, 'You shall not have that bit! Give it to me! You shall not have it! It is too good for such as you! I will have that bit! Give it to me!'

"And then both of them would run and push and shove, and squeak and squeal, and make such a noise and din, that there was no peace in the field; so that the don'key, when he found he could not eat his grass in peace, gave a loud bray, and ran up to the pigs.

"By his loud bray he meant to say to them, 'You bad pigs, be still, and do not make such a noise. If you run and push and shove, and squeak and squeal, and fight, and make such a noise and din, I shall find a way to make you keep still, which I can tell you you will not like.'

"But, when the pigs heard the don'key bray, they would

not mind him. 'He is on'ly a don'key,' thought they. 'If we choose to run and push and shove, and squeak, and make such a noise and din, who can stop us? Not that old don'key there. Let him try his best or his worst: we will do as we like, and run and push and shove, and squeak and squeal, and make as much noise and din as we please.'

"So the one gave a shove, and the oth'er gave a push, and the one gave a squeak, and.the other gave a squeal, till the poor don'key was half wild with all their noise and din. So he gave one more loud bray, as if to say, 'You bad pigs, you vex me too much. Why can you not eat your food in peace? then no one would have come near you to touch you or hurt you; but as you choose to push and shove, and squeak and squeal, you must be made to keep still in a way you will not like, for I can-not eat my grass in such a noise and din.'

"So the don'key went up to the pigs; and he took one pig by the ear, and he swung him up off the ground, and he swung him here, and he swung him there, and he swung him this way, and he swung him that, till the poor pig had hard'ly so much breath left as would help him to squeak.

"And then, when the don'key saw that the pig had hard'ly so much breath left as would help him to squeak, the don'key let him fall to the ground, and brayed once more, as if to say, 'There! I think I have taught you to be-have now. I do not think you can now push and shove, and squeak and squeal, and make such a noise and din. I think you will now let me eat my grass in peace.'

"And the don'key was right in that: the pigs had got such a fright, that not a sound did they make; but they ran from the don'key, and kept still, lest the don'key should come and take them by the ears, and swing them round to pun'ish them."

"Ah! they should have been wise, good pigs, and not have made such a noise. But is this a true sto'ry?"

"Yes, it is a true sto'ry. If the pigs had been good and still, they might have eat'en their fruit in peace, and the don'key would not have come near to hurt them."

——oo✸ːoo——

NOW LIST TO WHAT THE LAZY MAID TO BABY IN THE CRADLE SAID.

NIGHT and day I'm thinking
    Mine's a weary place;
With a fan I drive the flies
    From the baby's face.

While the rest are dancing gay,
I must by the cradle stay,
On its rocking fix my thought:
Sleep, you little good-for-nought!

Hark! I hear the music sound;
Now they all go round and round;
Here I mope, and here I sing:
Hush! you little fretful thing.

Was she not a bad maid to speak so to the dear little baby?

HOW THE PARROT MADE THE HORSE LOSE HIS LIFE.

"I HAVE one more tale to tell you; and this, too, is a true tale. In a large old town near the sea, there is a place they call the docks. In-to these docks the sea comes so that the ships can sail quite close up to where the stores are, in which the men wish to put the goods they have brought in their ships from all parts of the world.

"Now, as soon as a ship comes in-to the docks, men bring carts, and take all the bags and the bales and the casks out of the ship, and put them in-to the carts; and then the men take the carts to the stores where the bags and the bales and the casks are to go.

"Now, the horses which are put in these carts do not want the whip nor the rein to make them do what they are bid. They are so good they will do all that they are bid as soon as they are told. If the man says, 'Stand still,' they stand still, — so still! If the man says, 'Ho! back! back!' then back they go as soon as they are told.

"Now, near the docks there was an inn; and the man who kept the inn had a pet parrot, and her name was Poll. Poll would sit on her perch, and look at all that went on, and talk and talk, as plain as a man! and what she did hear the men say, Poll would say too; and Poll could say, 'Stand still,' and 'Ho! back! back!' as well as the men could.

"One day Poll saw a horse and cart quite near to her. There was no one with the horse and cart, for the man had gone to the inn to get some beer. Poll thought this would

23

be a fine time to have some fun; so she said, quite loud,
'Ho! back! back!'

"Back went the horse as he was bid; for the poor horse
thought it was the man who bid him go back. Poll thought
it was such good fun to see the horse do as he was bid, that
she said two or three times more, 'Ho! back! back!' And
the poor horse went back and back, as it was told.

"But Poll said, 'Ho! back! back!' once too often: for
the horse had gone back, back, back, till it had got to the
end of the wharf; and when Poll said, 'Ho! back! back!' the
last time, the horse went back with the cart in-to the sea.

"Oh, it was sad to look at the cart and the horse as they
fell in-to the sea! The men ran as fast as they could to try
to get the horse out of the sea, but it was all of no use.
They could not get the horse out of the sea, till the poor
thing was quite, quite dead."

"Oh, how sad! I wish the horse had stood still."

"Yes: was it not sad that the poor horse should die?"

"I wish Poll had said, 'Stand still.' It would have been
all right then."

"That it would. It was a sad thing that Poll did not say
the right word. It would be well that we should all think
of this; for we may do much harm if we do not say the
right word at the right time."

HOW THE DOG WOULD NOT QUIT HIS MASTER'S GOODS.

At the great fire in Que-bec, Oc-to'ber, 1866, a dog, whose name was Watch, was set to guard his mas'ter's things in a yard. The name of the mas'ter was Lee; and Mr. Lee said to the dog, "Now, Watch, be good, and do not let man or boy touch my things, which I leave in your charge."

Then Mr. Lee went to see to his wife and child, and Watch stood as a guard by the goods. But soon the fire grew to be quite a large fire; and it crept and crept and crept, on, on, on, till it came quite near to the place where Watch stood as guard by the goods.

Then some men and boys, who saw that the dog would be burnt if he did not leave the goods and run off fast, went near and said, "Come here, Watch; come here! Run, run, you poor dog, or you will be burnt to death."

But Watch thought they came to touch the goods; and so he did bark at them, and bark and bark, till they ran off. Then Watch thought the fire was quite hot: but still he would not leave the goods. Then a man came, and did try to drive him off; but Watch would not go.

He did bark at the man, as much as to say, "My mas'ter did tell me to stay here, and guard these goods; and here I mean to stay as long as I live, till my mas'ter comes, and calls me off." So poor Watch did stay and stay, though the heat was hard to bear: and by and by the fire got so near, that the flames were blown right in his face ; and then the good, true dog did howl with pain, and he thought, " Why does not my mas'ter come, and tell me I may go ? "

But the mas'ter could not come, for now the fire did rage so that no one could get near to the place where Watch kept guard by the goods. And so this good dog, this true dog, this brave dog, did stay there on guard, till the flames swept up, and burnt him to death. Was not that a sad end for poor Watch ?

WHY WILLY WANTS THE CURTAIN UP.

" Cold wind, cold wind ! you may rumble shrilly :
Snug and happy in his bed lies our little Willy.
Round moon, round moon ! on the snow you glisten :
You may hear our Willy laugh, if you will but listen."

" Bright stars, bright stars ! how the snow has drifted !
Mother, let the curtain stay, — let me have it lifted ;
For I like to see the stars, if awake I'm keeping,
And to have the stars see *me*, if I am a-sleeping."

SANDY BAY.

HOW A GOOSE DID LOVE A DOG.

ONCE there was a goose that loved a dog so much she would not quit the place where he was. She could not be made to go with the rest of the geese to roost by night. She would sit at the yard gate all day long in sight of the dog. When the dog went out of the yard, and ran to the woods or fields, this poor goose would run near him, and keep up with him by the help of her wings.

If the dog barked, she would run at the per'son the dog barked at. For two years she kept up this strange love for the dog. At last the dog fell ill. The goose would not quit his side, day nor night; no, not even to feed; and she might have starved to death if a pan of corn had not been put near her from which she could feed. The dog died; and then the goose would not take food. She did not live three weeks af'ter the dog died.

Now what do you think was the cause of the love of the poor goose for the dog? I will tell you; and you must bear in mind that this is not a made-up sto'ry; it is all true. It seems that once a sly old fox came to the yard, and sprang on the goose, and took her by the neck, and be-gan to drag her a-way that he might kill and eat her.

But the brave dog did bark, as much as to say, "You old thief of a fox, do you let that goose go, or I will give you fits. I will bite you, and shake you, and make you wish you had not shown your thief's face in our yard. Do you hear? Drop that goose." But the sly old fox did not mind the dog's bark.

The sly old fox thought to himself, 'What a nice din'ner

I shall make on this fine, fat goose! I will run so fast that that noisy dog can-not catch me. I will have a nice, good din'ner — I will." But, though the fox ran fast, he could not run with the goose in his mouth so fast as the dog could run with no goose. Soon the dog did get so near the fox as to spring right on him, and bite him by the throat till he let the poor goose go.

Then the fox ran off so fast that the dog gave up the chase, and came up to the goose to see if she had been much hurt. She was more scared than hurt; and the good dog did lick the place on her neck where the fox had bit her, — did lick it till she was quite well.

How glad the goose was! She could not talk; but she could say, " Quack, quack, quack," by which she meant, " You dear, good dog, you have saved my life; you have made that cru'el old fox let go his hold of me. He would have torn me, he would have killed me, he would have eat'en me for his din'ner, if you had not come up, and saved me. I shall love you all the rest of my life, you dear, brave dog!"

This was what the goose meant when she cried, " Quack, quack, quack." What did the dog say in re-ply? He could on'ly say, " Bow, wow;" by which he meant, " You are a good lit'tle goose, and I am glad I was nigh to save you from that sly old fox. I will kill him sure, the next time he sneaks in-to our yard."

And now you know why the goose did love this brave dog so much; and why, when the brave dog died, she did grieve and pine, and turn a-way from her food till she died too.* If a poor goose could be so grate'ful for a kind act, ought not we to show much love to our friends, and, most of all, to God, to whom we owe all the good of our lives?

* See the facts of this story in Willoughby's " Ornithology." The dog and goose belonged to Mr. William Sharpe of East Barnet, England.

SONGS FOR OUR PETS.

"Mamma," said Louisa, "you sent me to-day up stairs with the nurse and Willy to play; and I told her I thought it was both wrong and silly to say things like this to our dear little Willy:—

> 'Hey diddle diddle,
> The cat and the fiddle,
> The cow jumped over the moon ;
> The little dog laughed
> To see the fine sport,
> And the dish ran away with the spoon.'

"Nurse says she has found these rhymes of great use, for children are pleased to hear Mother Goose. Now can we not find, mother, something less silly, and both good and true, to amuse our dear Willy?"

"I think you are right," her mother replied; "nurse must try to amuse him with something beside. But babies are pleased with the jingle of rhyme, and old Mother Goose has been read a long time. Let us find little songs that are not quite so silly, and buy them for nurse to amuse little Willy. We give him each day fresh milk and sweet bread, and his dear little mind must be properly fed. 'Tis not easy to find sweet thoughts, good and true, in nursery rhymes that are pretty and true. Yet the Saviour did say, (and I wish we would read the saying, and heed it), 'My

lambs ye must feed.'   In this beautiful world, so joyous and
bright, there are many good things, of which poets might
write : the blue sky above us, the flowers and the trees, the
singing of birds, and the humming of bees.   Songs of these
could not fail to give the child pleasure, if written in simple
and sweet flowing measure.   Songs of these, let us hope,
without stint will be seen on the page of Miss Seaverns's
new Magazine."

OUR JOHN.

Our John is three years old.   He does not sleep now in
the day-time; but he goes to bed at six o'clock, and gets up
at four.   It is not light at that time, these cold days; so
Jane, the maid, lights a fire, and then John takes a bath.
See him in his tub, with one foot up and one foot down, and
his hands on the sides of the tub.

One day last week, John could not be found.   Twelve
o'clock came, but no one in the house had seen John since
nine o'clock.   " I think he must be at the black-smith's

shop," said Jane the maid; "for he likes to see the black-smith shoe the horses."

So Jane ran to the black-smith, but the black-smith said he had not seen John that day. "I think he must be a-sleep on the hay in the barn," said Ann the cook. So we ran to the barn; and first we looked in the cow's stall, and then in the horse's stall, and then in the hay-loft, but no John was to be seen.

"What shall we do?" said his mother. "I hope he has not fallen down the well." "I will ask Nep," said I. Nep is our old dog. So I took one of John's mittens, and held it to Nep's nose, and then led Nep to the well; but Nep shook his head, as if to say, "How silly to think that John is here! Come with me, and I will lead you to him!"

So Nep trotted off, and I went after him; and Nep put his nose down to the ground, and smelt and smelt, and then gave a bark, as if to say, "All right!" Then he ran down one street, and up another, till he came to a place where a crowd stood round a man who had lost both arms in battle.

The man had a box round his neck, into which the folks put money. The man's little daugh'ter played on a hand-organ. John was so pleased, he did not know how fast the time had gone by. I led him home, and he says he will not stay away again with-out leave. John has a tin soldier, who stands guard when John takes his bath. Can you not see him? John is to have a drum, but I hope he will not make too much noise with it. He means to learn to read, and be a good boy.

UNCLE CHARLES.

LULLABY FOR BABY.

Hush, little baby,
  I'll sing you a song;
One that is sweet,
  And not very long:
     Peep! peep!
     Go to sleep.

All the small birdies
  Are snugly a-sleep;
No more must baby
  Wide a-wake keep:
     Peep! peep!
     Go to sleep.

Lullaby, baby!
  Taking your rest;
Nothing shall harm you,
  Safe in your nest:
     Peep! peep!
     Go to sleep.

WAKING SONG FOR BABY.

Up from the water
  Comes the red sun;
Baby is stirring,
  Day is begun:
     Wake! rise!
     Baby cries.

Hear what a chatter
  All the birds make;
Even the moolly-cow
  Now is a-wake:
     Wake! rise!
     Baby cries.

Baby is hungry,
  He must be fed;
Wash him and dress him;
  Wake, sleepy-head!
     Wake! rise!
     Baby cries.

DO NOT TEASE A LION.

ONE day last June, we went to a large tent, to see the wild beasts. In one cage there were two male lions. In another cage there was a mother lion, with two young ones. We call a mother lion, a *lioness*. Each of these young ones was about the size of a large cat.

The keeper took them out of their cage, and let us play with them; for they did not try to bite or scratch. The lioness was glad to have us play with her young lions; but,

if one of them gave a cry, she would start up, and look to
see that we did not hurt them. When she saw that we were
good and kind to them, she would lie down, and purr like a
big cat.

James had brought a flask of milk and a bowl; and we
poured out the milk in the bowl, and fed the young lions.
You should have seen them lap up the milk. James took
one of them in his arms, and held him for some time.

While we stood there playing with the young lions, we
heard a loud cry; and, looking round, we saw a large boy,
whose left foot had been caught by the claw of one of the
old male lions. This boy, whose name was Ralph, had been
told that he must not tease the lions. There was a large
printed card over the cage, telling folks not to go near the
bars of the cage.

But this rash boy, when he saw that the keeper was not
looking, began to tease the lions by kicking at the bars of
their cage. At first they were too proud to heed him; and
this made Ralph fool with them all the more. By and by
one of the lions gave a growl. This should have been a
warning to Ralph to stop his fooling; but he did not stop.

He gave one more kick, and it was his last; for one of
the lions caught him by the left foot and held him tight.
How Ralph did scream! The keep'er ran to see what was
the matter. He found that Ralph had started back with
terror and with pain. The boy stood on his right foot, while
his left was held fast by the lion, who was growl'ing fierce'ly.
Ralph's hat had fallen off in his fright.

He could not draw away his boot from the lion's claw; but
the keep'er was a'ble to draw Ralph's foot out of the boot,
by leaving the boot in the claws of the lion, who quick'ly
drew it in'to his cage, and, ly'ing down, be-gan growl'ing
over it, and soon tore it to pieces.

The bad boy's foot was much hurt; for the lion's claws had gone through the leath'er of the boot, and, in dragging the foot out, the flesh was torn. The boy's friends had to put him in a coach, and take him home, for he was in too much pain to walk.

For more than a week he had to lie on a bed, with his foot bound up in strips of cloth. He is now quite well, and I think you may be sure he will not again kick at the bars of a lion's cage.

We ought not to tease dumb beasts. We ought not to tease even those that cannot hurt us. A good horse may be spoilt by the tricks which a foolish stable boy will play on him. The child who would give pain to a fly or a worm should be made to see what a sin it is. I love to see a child kind to dumb beasts. I love to see a child give help even to a drown'ing fly. God will not hold that child guilt'less who hurts even the mean'est in'sect, when there is no need of doing it harm.

DAISY DAY AND THE MOUSE.

Sit down, and I will tell you a true story of Daisy Day and a mouse. Daisy Day was a little girl, not four years old; and her father was Mr. Day, who had a small farm not far from New York. Once, when the air was soft and warm, Daisy sat down on a rock, near the old barn. She had a bun in her hand; and, as she ate the bun, the crumbs fell on her lap.

As she sat there, the birds came, and sang sweetly in the tree that bent over her head: The wind blew the scent of new-made hay in her face. The bees came buzzing close to her hair, as much as to say, "That's you, is it, Daisy? How do you do? You need not fear us."

"Oh, no! I do not fear you," thought Daisy. "I know, if I do not hurt you, you will not hurt me: so go and get as much honey as you can, you busy bees; for I am so sleepy, I do not know what to do."

"Buzz, buzz!" said the bee, and flew up to the lime-tree which was in bloom over head. Then Daisy leaned her back against the trunk of the tree, and fell asleep.

While she slept, a wee mouse peeped out from a hole under the old barn. It was a young mouse, whose mother had sent it forth to earn its own living. The times were hard in Mouse-land. Old Pop, the barn cat, kept such a strict watch, that a mouse could not run to pick up a grain of corn, without the risk of being caught.

The mother mouse, as she sent forth the young mouse from the hole, made two or three squeaks, which may have meant, "Now, take care of old Pop, the cat, my dear Pee-wee; for he is on the watch all the time, and he will run to seize you if you do not take care."

"Squeak, squeak!" said little Pee-wee; and I think, if he could have told what he meant in words, he would have said, "O mother! I see little Daisy Day fast asleep under the lime-tree; and, oh, dear! such a lot of nice crumbs as are in her lap!—crumbs enough to give all our folks a good dinner! Hush! I will creep and creep and creep, slow, slow, slow, till I can run up her lap, and taste of those nice crumbs."

So what did Pee-wee do, but look all round to see if Pop, the cat, was near by. Ah! Pop was hid be-hind a bush; and, though Pee-wee could not see Pop, Pop could see Pee-wee. And Pop may have thought to her-self, "Halloo!

there's a mouse going to steal crumbs ! I will wait till I get a good chance, and then I will rush out, and catch him, and eat him up."

Out from the hole crept Pee-wee; but he had not gone ten steps, when a leaf fell in his path, and made him start so, that he ran back. Then out he crept once more, near and more near, till he came to Daisy Day's left foot. It was a pretty little foot, so far as he could see, hid as it was in a neat little black shoe and a red sock.

Pee-wee put one of his fore-feet on the shoe, and then put his other foot on the little red sock. Daisy did not stir; but old Pop, the cat, lay quivering like a snake, all ready for a spring. Pee-wee would have run back to his hole if he had known that Pop was so near; but the poor little mouse was so hungry! Near and more near he crept; and at last up he ran a-long Daisy's little blue frock, right into her lap. Was he not a bold little mouse?

" I will have you now, you little thief!" thought old Pop; but Pee-wee only saw the crumbs. " Oh, what a feast I shall have !" thought the poor little mouse. " I do not think this good little Daisy would hurt me if she were to wake and see me ; for I have known her to help a toad that was hurt, and the bees all seem to like her."

So Pee-wee ate a crumb. How nice it was! Then he ate another; and still Daisy kept on sleeping. But just then Pee-wee heard a noise which made him shudder. He knew that old Pop was coming. Oh, dear! oh, dear! What should Pee-wee do? It was a long way back to his hole. The fierce cat would catch him, and eat him up, if he should try to run a-way.

" I know what I will do," thought Pee-wee at last. " I will trust to little Daisy Day to save me from old Pop." Then what do you sup-pose the little mouse did? Why, just as old Pop made a spring, and land'ed in Daisy's lap, Pee-wee ran up, and hid him-self snug in Daisy's bosom.

"Why! what is this?" cried Daisy, waking up at once. "Old cat, what do you want in my lap? And what is this little warm, trembling thing in my bosom?"—"Squeak, squeak, squeak!" said a little voice in re-ply.

"I declare, it is a mouse — a poor little fright'ened mouse!" said Daisy Day; and she began to laugh. Then she put up her hand, soft, soft, and patted the mouse. Then she shook off Pop, and cried, "S'cat, S'cat! Go off, old Pop! You shall not have this dear little mouse. It is my mouse now. It ran to me for help, and I mean to take care of it."

"Mew, mew! yeow, yeow!" cried Pop, as much as to say, "Give me up that mouse. I must have that mouse. I want to eat that mouse." But Daisy Day stamped her foot till Pop crept off. Then Daisy ran into the house, and put little Pee-wee in an empty cage, and fed him with bread and milk.

In a few weeks the little mouse grew so tame, that Daisy could let him out of his cage to run a-bout the room. She put a red silk cord round his neck. He knew her voice so well, that he would run to her when she called him. He would play with her as a kitten plays. She had a baby-house; and he would go in, and lie down on a mat in the best parlor. Is not this a nice story of Daisy Day and the little mouse Pee-wee?

But Daisy had to take great care lest Pop should get at Pee-wee. She made the door of the little house very small, so that Pee-wee could run in, but Pop could not follow. Pee-wee was safe in the little house; and Pop could stay outside, and cry, "mew," but could not enter.

EMILY CARTER.

HOW THE KITTENS TOOK CARE OF THE FRUIT.

" Look at that bird!   What has it in its mouth?"

" I think it has a bit of a plum.   I saw it fly to the tree, and I think it went to get a bit of a plum.   Birds love fruit, and it is hard to keep them from it.   Shall I tell you how a friend of mine kept the birds off from her fruit?"

" Yes, do! since it is true, I would like to hear it."

" My friend had some fine large straw'ber-ry beds in her gar'den, and the fruit was fine and large and sweet and good.   But the birds knew this quite as well as my friend did ; and they would fly quite close to the beds, and hop, hop, hop up to the fruit, and pick a bit here, and pick a bit there, till my friend found, that, if she did not put a stop to their bad ways, she should lose all her fruit.

" Now, my friend had a fine white cat, and this cat had five white kit'tens.   So my friend thought, ' What if I make the kittens take care of the fruit?' "

" The kittens take care of the fruit!   How could they do that ?"

. " Wait, and you shall hear.   My friend had five small huts made.   Each hut was just as big as a kitten would want. And she put the huts near to the beds of fruit, and then she put one little kitten in each little hut; and she tied each lit'tle kitten to a nice long chain, so that the kitten could run out of its hut, and play and jump and frisk as much as it liked, but could not run far away.

" And my friend put a nice soft rug in each little hut, so that each little kitten might have a nice soft bed to lie down on ; and then she put a nice little plate of good sweet milk

39

by the side of each little hut, so that each little kitten might
have as much as it liked to drink; and then she put each
little kit'ten in its own little hut, and told it to be a good
little kitten, and take care of the fruit, and not let the birds
come near to harm nor to eat it.

"Now, when the five little kittens were left in their five
lit'tle huts, they be-gan to purr and to mew, as if to say,
'We will be good little kittens — such good little kittens!
We will take care of the fruit; and we will not let, no, not so
much as one bird come near to harm nor to eat it.'

"So these little kittens sat at the doors of their little
huts; and, when they saw the birds come near the fruit, out
they would run and jump and spring, and put up their backs
and spit, and put up their tails and purr.   And when the
birds saw the little kittens run and jump and spring, and
put up their backs and spit, and put up their tails and purr,
the birds were in fear, oh, such great fear! and they would
hop and hop and hop, and fly and fly and fly.

"'What can these white things be?' thought the birds,
—'these things which run and jump and spring, and put
up their backs and spit, and put up their tails and purr?   If
we go too near those white things, who can tell but that,
when we go to eat the fruit, they may eat us for our pains?
So we will hop and hop and hop, and fly and fly and fly, to
get out of the way of those five white things.'

"So the little kittens took such care of the fruit, that not
a bird came near to harm nor to eat it; and my friend had
all the fruit that she wanted, and the kittens had all the
milk that they wanted, and the birds had not one bit of the
fruit."

"But I would like to have had the poor birds eat some of
the fruit; would not you?   The birds do good as well as
harm.   They keep off the bugs."

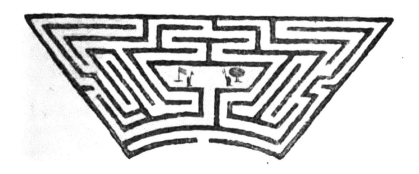

WILL YOU WALK INTO MY GARDEN?

HERE is a plan of my garden. The lines show the hedges. The white spaces between the lines are the walks. Some folks say it is a great puzzle for them to find their way to the middle of my garden. Some say that it is quite as hard for them to get out as to get in. Well, my walks are meant for a puzzle; and, if you do not like to be puzzled, you must not go into my garden.

You must not go in, unless you mean to find your way to the middle, where you see the two men with flags. If you go in, you must not turn back. You must keep on till you come to the flags; and you must not cross any of the lines. You must keep in the white path between the lines. I do not let folks climb over my hedge. My hedge is five feet high.

But I will tell you what you can do. You can take a pin or a pencil, and trace out on the plan the way you would go, if I were to let you walk to the middle of my garden. Remember, you must not cross the lines. Now look at the plan, and see if you can get to the middle without crossing any of the lines. How would you go? Which of the walks would you take?

Last week a little boy, whose name is Walter Gray, came to me to know if he might walk to the middle of my garden. I told him he might do it, if he could. He said he would try. Off he went, and for an hour I did not hear any thing of him. At the end of that time I heard a cry of "Ho! ho! ho! I can't find my way out! Help me, somebody, to find my way out! I found my way in, but I cannot find my way out. Ho! ho! ho!"

Then I knew what the matter was. But, as I was busy, I called to my old dog Nap, and said, "Hark, Nap! What is that noise?" Nap could not speak; but he barked, as much as to say, "That little boy has lost his way in the garden. Shall I go and show him the way out?" "Go!" said I. So Nap ran, and in two minutes he brought the little boy out; and the little boy was glad, and laughed to think he had been helped out by a dog.

UNCLE CHARLES.

HOW THE CAT KNEW ANN FROM JANE.

"Do you think that cats grow as fond of those who are kind to them as dogs do?"

"I do not know if all cats do so. Some cats have quite as strong a love for their friends as dogs have: of that I am quite sure. When my Aunt Ann was young, she and my Aunt Jane had a pet cat. Both were kind to the cat, and the cat was fond of them both; but it was of my Aunt Ann he was most fond. When Ann was in the room, Muff would not go to Jane; no, not if Jane held out a plate of nice meat, or a cup with sweet cream, and said, 'Muff, this is for you if you will come to me.' Muff would look up, and put out his nose, and sniff; and then he would jump up in Ann's lap, and look up in her face, and purr, as if he would like to say, if he could, 'Meat is good, and cream is good; but you are better than meat or cream. I love you best, and I shall stay with you.' And then Muff would roll him-self in'to a ball in Aunt Ann's lap, and no one could make him stir till Aunt Ann put him down on the ground.

"Now Ann and Jane slept in the same room. Each had a bed for her-self, one on this side the room, and one on that. And, as soon as it was light, Muff would come and sit down by the door; and, when the maid came to tell Aunt Ann and Aunt Jane it was time to get up, Muff would go in'to the room with her, and jump on Ann's bed, and come and rub his nose on her hand or her face, and purr, purr-r, purr-r-r, as much as to say, 'How do you do? Have you had a good sleep? I am so glad to see you once more!'

"But Muff did not go to say, 'How do you do?' to Aunt Jane; though he would purr out his thanks if she came and said, 'How do you do?' to him. One night when they went to bed, Aunt Jane said to Aunt Ann, 'If you were to sleep in my bed, and I in yours, do you think Muff would know which was which? I think he would come and rub his nose on me then, and not on you.'—'I do not think he would,' said Aunt Ann; 'but we will try.'

"So Aunt Ann slept in Aunt Jane's bed, and Aunt Jane in Aunt Ann's. Next day Muff came in'to the room with the maid; and he ran to Ann's bed, and with a great jump he was at once by the side of Jane. Then Muff made a sad cry,—oh, such a sad cry!—as much as to say, 'Oh! where is my dear Ann? Where is my dear Ann gone?'

"And Muff would not so much as give one purr, nor rub his head once on the hand Jane held out to him. But he gave one great jump, and ran off to the bed at the far side of the room; and when he saw his dear friend Ann was in that bed, — oh! who so glad as Muff? He jumped, and he purred, as if he did not know how best to show his joy.

"He rubbed his head up and down Ann's face, and up and down Ann's arm, and looked at her as if he would ask, 'Why did you play me such a trick? Did you think I should not know my own Ann? Oh! how came you to think Muff was such a fool? Why, Muff would know Ann out of all the world. Do not do this a-gain. It makes Muff sad to think you should play him such a trick as this.'

"'Dear old Muff!' said Aunt Ann. 'Yes, it was too bad, was it not, to play you such a trick? You are a dear, good old Muff; and it was a shame to try and take you in. I will do so no more.' And then Muff would purr, as much as to say, 'Oh, I love you so much, — so much! I love you more than cake or meat or milk or cream, or all the good things that there are in the world."

THE WILD VINE AND THE CLOVER.

"We sprang together from the clod,"
　　A Wild Vine to the Clover said:
"How little thou hast gained in height,
　　Whilst I wave proudly overhead!"

The Clover to the taunt replied,
　　And still her cheerful bearing kept,
"Nay, do not boast, I'm quite content;
　　For I have *stood* while thou hast *crept.*"

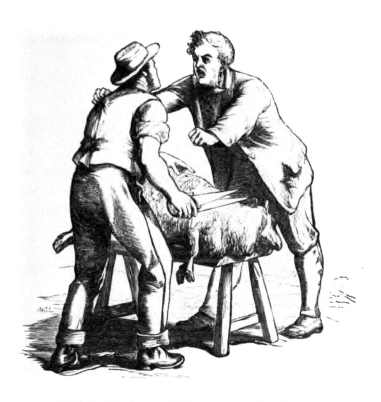

HOW TIM AND TOM DID NOT AGREE.

Look at these two men. They seem to be having a quarrel. The face of one of them is ugly with anger. I will tell you a story of these two men.

They were brothers, and the name of one of them was Tim, and of the other Tom. Their father died, and left them a flock of sheep.

Now, if these brothers had been good and kind, they might have kept their sheep, and made much gain by them, and lived in peace. But Tim and Tom could not agree.

If Tim said, " Let us put the sheep in the field by the wood," Tom would say, " No: let us keep them in the field on the hill." Then Tom would say, " No: the feed is poor in the field on the hill." To which Tim would reply, " The field by the wood must be kept for mowing."

Tim would then say, " I have as much right as you have to say where the sheep shall be kept. They are as much mine as yours." And Tom would reply, " I know more about sheep than you do, and I am three years older."

" I don't care for that," Tim would say. " You want to have your way all the time, and I will not put up with it. I will show you that I know how to take care of my rights."

And so these two brothers would keep up the quarrel. From morning to night, you could hear nothing but cross words from their lips. At last, Tom said to Tim, " Since we cannot live in peace, let us divide the flock. Half of the sheep shall be mine, and half shall be yours."

To this Tim agreed. But, when they came to divide the flock, there was one odd sheep. What should they do with that? " Let us toss up a cent for it," said Tom: " if the cent comes down head up, the odd sheep shall be mine; if not, it shall be yours."

" I will do no such thing," said Tim. " Let us kill the sheep, and then halve it." But Tom wanted some wool for a pair of stockings; so he said, " First let me shear off its wool. Let me shear it now." — " You shall not shear it!" cried Tim. " It is as much my sheep as it is yours, and I say the shears shall not touch it."

" I will shear my half of this sheep any how," said Tom; " and then you can shear your half when you please." And so Tom began to shear his half of the sheep, though Tim all the while scolded Tom for doing it.

When it was done, the sheep ran off up the hill, and the two brothers went home full of anger. That night there was a storm; and the poor sheep was caught by a gust of wind, and swept from a high cliff, and was found the next day, dead and cold on the plain below.

"Brother Tom," said Tim, "if you had not shorn that sheep, it would not have died of the cold. It is frozen, all through having been shorn by you." — "Not so," said Tim. "The wind caught it, and threw it over the cliff, because only one-half of the fleece was shorn. If you had shorn your half, as you ought to have done, the sheep would have kept its balance, and would not have been blown from the cliff."

"No such thing!" said Tim. "You must pay me for my half 'of that sheep, or I will go to law about it."

"Not a cent will I pay you," said Tim. "I am the one who ought to be paid."

So the two brothers went to law about the sheep. "What a nice case!" said the lawyers, rubbing their hands, and then holding them out for a fee. Tim and Tom paid large sums to the lawyers, and the case was kept in court five years. At the end of that time, Tim and Tom found they had parted with all their money, and all their flocks of sheep, and were ruined in purse and in credit.

See the folly of strife! These brothers found at last, but too late, that they had lost their peace of mind, and their money, through their quarrelsome habits.

Tim and Tom were foolish, but not much more so than two boys I know of. I will not tell you their names, for I think they are now ashamed of what they did. Their father had bought for them a pony; but how did they act?

When John wanted to ride, then Henry would say, "No, I must ride now." And, when Henry wanted to ride, John would say, "No, let me ride first." The father, finding that his gift was thus made a cause of strife, sold the pony, and the foolish boys had no nice rides after that.

SANDY BAY.

THE BOY WITH A WHIP.

Do you see this small boy with the whip?
Yes, he has both a whip and a sword.
He has the whip in his right hand,
But the sword is hung a-cross his breast.
In his left hand, see, he holds a string.
Tell me what you see tied to the string.
Tied to the string I see a small toy-horse.
On the back of the horse I see a doll.
Three nine-pins and a ball lie on the floor.
Do not hit us, boy, with the lash of the whip.
If you do not mind, the doll will fall off,
But I do not think she will be hurt much.

48

E F G H

E   Edwin enters with a nest of eggs.

F   Fanny has a basket full of flowers.

G   Grace and Gertrude look at the grapes.

H   Henry hands hazel-nuts to Harriet.

For other Letters, see pages 17, 73.

A CHASE TO TAKE BACK A BAD WORD.

OLD MAN.

I SEE a boy running as fast as he can :
Now, what are you running for, my little man ?

LITTLE BOY IN BLUE.

If you please, my good sir, do not stop me or stay:
I shall lose what I'm running for, if I delay.

OLD MAN.

You are quite out of breath with your race, little master;
So stop here and rest: you can then run the faster.

LITTLE BOY IN BLUE.

Ah, no ! in my chase I shall never succeed
If for only one moment I slacken my speed.

OLD MAN.

But what is the matter that thus you must run ?
Say, is it an errand ? or is it for fun ?

LITTLE BOY IN BLUE.

Not for fun !   There's no fun in the act which I rue.

OLD MAN.

Then tell me, what is it, my little boy blue ?

LITTLE BOY IN BLUE.

To tell you, good sir, I'm not willing to-day ;
So please step aside, and move out of my way.

50

OLD MAN.

Perhaps I can help you, my little boy blue ;
So tell me your trouble without more ado.

LITTLE BOY IN BLUE.

To my brother I spoke, sir, an angry, bad word :
Oh ! what would I give if it had not been heard !

OLD MAN.

And pray tell me, what are you trying to do
By running in this way, my little boy blue ?

LITTLE BOY IN BLUE.

That word I would catch : I am now on its track.
Oh ! help me to seize it, to take it quite back.

OLD MAN.

My little boy blue, the good racer Eclipse
Could never catch up with that word from your lips.

LITTLE BOY IN BLUE.

And is there no help, when that word I so rue ?

OLD MAN.

Only this : Say, " Forgive me ! " my little boy blue.

LITTLE BOY IN BLUE.

Oh ! that I will say ; for my brother I love.

OLD MAN.

What more ?

LITTLE BOY IN BLUE.

Say, " Forgive me, O Father above ! "

EMILY CARTER.

"ONLY A LITTLE BROOK."

A few weeks ago, a dear lit'tle girl in Bath, Maine, was so ill that she felt she could no long'er live in her poor, suf'fer-ing body. At first she was sad at the thought. It did seem to her such a long, strange, dark way, from the warm room where she was with her friends, to the heav'en where Christ is, and where those who are good and pure in this life shall find a home much bet'ter than any on this earth!

But soon this lit'tle girl be-gan to think, and to feel that God must be just as near to her in the hour of death, and in the room where she lay, as he had been in the hour of her birth; that, as she owed her life in this world to him, she must owe her life in the next to him too; that so he must be just as near to her on the earth as in heav'en; and that his arms would be round a-bout her soul, and save it from harm when it left the dead bo'dy, no mat'ter where she might be.

As these thoughts came to her mind, a sweet smile stole o'ver her face. No more did she feel a-fraid'. She felt as if God's an'gels were quite near, to help and cheer her, and show her the way. She grew calm and happy. What at first had seemed to her a long, dark road, now seemed short and bright and ver'y near. And at last she cried out, *"Oh, it is on'ly a lit'tle brook!"* and so passed on to the heav'en-ly shore.

But what did she mean by *"on'ly a lit'tle brook"?* She meant that the way from our own world to the world where the soul goes when the body dies is not far; that, when we are good, God is as near to us in the world where we now are as he will be in the next; and that to pass from this life to the next is just like cross'ing a lit'tle brook, so shal'low that chil'dren can wade a-cross it, or sail their ti'ny boats on it.

Oh! how much do those men lose who do not be-lieve fully in that bet'ter life af'ter this, and who do not act as if they be-lieved it! Let us but mind the words of Christ, — be pure and good, and show love to God and man in our acts here; and then, like the lit'tle girl in Bath, Maine, we need not be a-fraid to have our bodies die; for there is no more cause for fear than in cross'ing a brook from one bank to another. Let us think of this when we say our little hymn, —

> " Now I lay me down to sleep,
> I pray the Lord my soul to keep :
> If I should die before I wake,
> I pray the Lord my soul to take."

ANNA LIVINGSTON.

THE BOY WHO DID A KIND ACT.

A TRUE STORY.

I KNOW a man of wealth whose first name is John. He lives in New York. He is a good man. He has giv'en large sums of mon'ey to help poor children. He was once a poor child him-self.

His par'ents died when he was ten years old. They had taught him to read and write, and, what is bet'ter still, to be good and hon'est and kind. But there was no one to take care of him; and one day he went forth to seek for work.

How hard it was for him to find any one to give him work! He asked of this man and of that. Ah! they none of them had any work to give him. At last he came to the store of Mr. Burns, who was a rich man, and, at that time, very busy. He was think'ing of his ships when John came into the room.

"What do you want, boy?" asked Mr. Burns. "If you please, sir, I want a place." — "I can'not do any thing for you," said Mr. Burns; "for, if I tried to do for all the boys who come to me for work, I could not find time to do any work for myself."

John made a bow, and left the room. Mr. Burns went to the win'dow, and stood there lost in thought. It was a bit'ter cold day. The wind blew. Snow and ice lay hard on the ground. Not far off he saw a horse and cart. The horse's blan'ket had been blown off, and the poor horse stood shiv'er-ing in the cold.

"I wish some one would take care of that poor horse!"

thought Mr. Burns. While he looked, a lit'tle boy took up the blan'ket, and fixed it nice'ly on the horse's back, and then pat'ted him ten'der-ly, as if say'ing, "Poor old fel'low! It is too bad to leave you here in the cold."

"That must be a good, kind boy," thought Mr. Burns; and he threw up the win'dow, and called to him. It was John, the poor or'phan boy. He came back to Mr. Burns. "My boy," said Mr. Burns, "I will find a place for you in my store. You shall not want work any more." John's for'tune be-gan there. Though rich now, he does not let man or beast suf'fer, if he can help it, for want of a blan'ket.

WILLIAM C. GODWIN.

THE LITTLE LIE-A-BED.

ANDY is an idler, loves to lie in bed :
Go and pull the pillow from beneath his head;
Pull the sheet and blanket from his sleepy eyes.
See, the sun is shining! Lazy-bones, arise!

While in stupid snoozing you are lying here,
We, our shovels using, make the side-walks clear;
With our sleds and baskets we take off the snow,
Till our cheeks and fingers all are in a glow.

Breakfast now is ready, yet in bed you lie :
O you little slug'gard! See, the sun is high!
We have learned our lessons, we've had work and play.
We've got health and wisdom from the new-born day.

EMILY CARTER.

JULIA TO HER DOLL.

Come out in the garden, my lady,—
  Come out in the garden with me:
I know a place lovely and shady,
  Where we two quite happy can be;
And there, by the fresh blooming flowers,
  With roses and lilies so sweet,
We will play all the bright noonday hours:
  Come! move now your nice little feet.

You are dressed in the mode, dear, believe me:
  Your bonnet, your skirt, and your waist,
If the fashion-plates do not deceive me,
  Are all in the latest good taste.
So come, show your figure, my lady,
  And put out your gay little feet:
Come where it is lovely and shady,—
  Come where all the flowers are sweet.

ANNA LIVINGSTON.

HOW THE DOG WOULD NOT TOUCH HIS FOOD TILL HIS MASTER SAID HE MIGHT.

"How fond Mr. Day seems of his dog!"

"Yes; does he not? and his dog is fond of him too. Mr. Day once told me a story of his dog, which shows how fond of him his dog is, and how he does just as Mr. Day bids him to do."

"Tell me that story if you please."

"Well, Mr. Day says, that, when he is at home, he puts a

plate of meat on the stone step of the house the last thing at night, that Tim (for that is the dog's name) may have a good meal; and Tim knows that his meal will be there for him, and the last thing at night Tim runs to the step, and waits and waits and waits, till the plate is brought out.

"But one night Mr. Day had so much to do, he did not give a thought to feeding poor Tim; and Tim waited and waited, and no nice meat was brought out for him. So by and by poor Tim must have thought to himself, 'There is no meat for me this night: I must go to bed without my food; but I do want my food so much!—oh, so much!'

"So Tim went off to his bed. But, just as Mr. Day had made up his mind to go to bed too, he thought! 'Why! Tim has not had his food. Poor Tim! he must want his supper.'

"So Mr. Day took the plate of meat and bones to the room where Tim slept. Now, when Tim heard his step in the room, Tim was glad, oh, so glad! for he wanted his food badly; and he jumped up so high,—so high, that he shook the plate, and some of the meat fell out on the floor.

"'Be still, Tim! be still!' said Mr. Day. 'See! you make a mess on the floor.' But Tim wanted his food so much, that he could not be still; and, for all Mr. Day said, he kept jumping and jumping all the more.

"So Mr. Day took a stick, and beat the dog, to show him he must not jump when he was told to stand still, but that he must do as he was bid: and then Mr. Day put the plate of meat near the dog's bed, but he did not look at Tim, nor did he say good-night to Tim, nor did he pat Tim; but he just put the plate of meat on the floor, and then he went to his own room, and went to bed.

"By and by he heard a cry,—such a sad, sad cry! At first he could not think what the cry was; at last he thought, 'That must be Tim. What can make Tim cry now? He did not cry when I beat him: what can make him cry now?'

"So Mr. Day lay still in his bed for a time; but still the cry went on, — a soft, low cry, which it was sad to hear. So Mr. Day got up, and went to the room where he had left Tim: and there stood the poor dog by the side of the plate of meat, with his nose on the plate; but he had not touched a bit— no, not so much as a bit, though he wanted food so much.

"And when he saw Mr. Day he ran up to him, and wagged his tail, and then he ran back to the plate, and then he looked up in his master's face, as much as to say, 'May I eat this now? I am good now. I will stand still. You went to bed, and you did not pat Tim, and you did not say, Eat it, Tim: so I do not know if I may eat it or not. May I eat it now; for I am good now, and I do want my food so much?'

"'Poor old Tim!' said Mr. Day: 'so you did not know if you might have your meat. Yes, Tim, you may have your meat.' And with that Mr. Day patted Tim on the head, and said, 'Good-night, good old dog, eat your meat.'

"And Tim did not wait to be twice told. As soon as he heard 'Eat your meat,' he set to work with such a right good will, that, by the time Mr. Day was once more in bed, I do not think there could have been much meat left in the plate."

"And if Mr. Day had not gone to see Tim, to say to him, 'You may eat your meat,' do you think Tim would have eaten no food that night?"

"I am quite sure Tim would have eaten no food. He would not have eaten so much as a bit till his master gave him leave."

"Poor old Tim! I am glad Mr. Day went to see him, and told him he might eat his food."

WHAT THE OLD CLOCK SAW AND HEARD.

TICK, tock, tick!
Our poor little Tommy is sick.
    He ate a mince-pie,
    And that makes him cry:
So come, Dr. Jollup, come quick!

Tock, tick, tock!
A knock! Do you hear it? A knock!
    The doctor is near:
    Now run, Susan dear,
Go, hurry, the door to unlock.

Tick, tock, tick!
"This boy," says the doctor, "is sick:
    So bring me a mug,
    And I'll mix him a drug
That shall make him as sound as a brick."

Tock, tick, tock!
"At your physic," says Tommy, "I mock;
    For gone is my ache,
    And no drug will I take:
You shall find me as firm as a rock."

Tick, tock, tick!
Says Jollup, "You serve me a trick!"
    Says Tommy, "Your drugs
    I throw to the bugs:
Now go, Dr. Jollup, go quick!"

EMILY CARTER.

HOW WE WENT TO SKATE.

I AM a small boy. My name is Edwin Drake. Not far from our house is a riv'er. It is now fro'zen so hard, that you can skate on it for ten miles. I love to skate. I have two broth'ers and two sis'ters. They are all old'er than I am. I am six years old.

May I tell you of a good time we had last week? It was a fine, calm day. The sun shone; but it was not so hot as to melt the snow. The wind did not blow. School did not keep. Moth'er said we might put on our skates and go six miles up the stream to a place we call Ce'dar Point.

How glad we all were! My sis'ters Kate and Laura can skate quite as well as John and Frank can. So we all put on our skates, and went down to the riv'er over the hard snow. Moth'er had put some cold chick'en and some bread and but'ter in a bas'ket, and John had tied the bas'ket on to his sled; for we meant to take din'ner at Ce'dar Point.

I could not skate quite as well as the rest; but they would skate a mile, and then come back to meet me. John cut his name on the ice two or three times. What a hap'py time we had! Our dog Train went with us. He had to run fast to keep up with us; but he seemed to like the sport as much as we did. How he did bark!

We left home at nine o'clock; and we got to Ce'dar Point at half-past ten. We might have got there at ten if we had not stopped to play by the way. Train tried to catch a poor lit'tle rab'bit; but we called him off. Kate said, "While we are so gay, we will not even make a poor rab'bit sad."

61

I will now tell you what we did when we got to Ce'dar
Point. We cut down some trees, and made a good fire on
a rock by the bank. Then we made seats, and sat down
be-fore the fire and ate our din'ner; for we were all hun'gry
by this time.

As we sat there, some lit'tle snow-birds came round us.
They were fat little things. Their feath'ers seemed quite
soft, and were of the col'or of a mouse's skin. We threw to
them some crumbs of bread. At first they were shy, and
would not come near; but, when they found we were their
good friends, they came and ate up the crumbs.

All at once — bang! — we heard the sound of a gun.
We all start'ed up. Old Train be-gan to bark. Then we
saw a man with a gun come from the wood. He had taken
aim at a fine duck on the ice. Here is a pic'ture of the duck.

I was glad when I found that the man with the gun had
not hurt the duck. High, high up in the air, the duck flew,
till it went far out of sight. It made a shrill cry as it rose.
The man with the gun came and sat down by our fire, and
we gave him some of our din'ner.

Then we went once more on the ice; and John taught me
to skate backward, and to make curves so as to cut the let-
ter S on the smooth ice. Laura sat down on the sled, and
Frank dragged her a mile, and back. All at once we heard

the sound of a horn. It was one that John had brought with him; but he had not let us see it. The sound meant, " It is time to go home."

So we put out the fire, and threw the crumbs and the bones where the poor birds could find them; and then we started for home. We found a weak place in the ice, but we did not fall through. We took sticks, and drove a ball along the ice. It was five o'clock when we got home. We were all tired. We took our suppers, and went to bed. We slept well that night. I hope we shall have one more good frolic on the ice before the winter ends.

THE RABBITS.

AMONG the sand-hills,
  Close by the sea,
The wild gray rabbits
  Were seen by me.

They live in burrows
  With winding ways,
And there they shclter
  On rainy days.

The mother-rabbits
  Make cosey nests,
With furry linings
  Got from their breasts.

The tender young ones
  Are nursed and fed,
And safely hidden
  In this snug bed.

And, when they're older,
  They all come out
Upon the sand-hills
  To frisk about.

They play, and nibble
  The coarse, dry grass;
But off they scamper
  When people pass.

THE PET OF THE VILLAGE.

THIS little girl lives in a village not ten miles from the Ohio River. Her first name is Emma. I do not know whether she will like to have me tell you the rest of her name. She is three years old, and I will tell you of a kind act she did on New Year's Day.

Her uncle gave her a dollar to spend for Christmas; and what do you think she did? Why, as she went to the shop to buy toys, she met a poor woman with a baby. They had been burned out of their house the night before. The baby needed clothes. So Emma gave the dollar to the poor woman, and felt more glad than if she had bought toys. She did another good thing; but, I will not tell you of it now.*

* If you must know what it was, see the 2d page of our cover.

64

GETTING READY FOR SCHOOL.

HERE they are! Henry, Frank, Laura, and little John, all ready to go to school! Their mother, Mrs. Ray, sees that John has his cape well buttoned up. Then she kisses him, and bids Laura take him by the hand, and lead him to school.

"Come, Henry," says Mrs. Ray, "leave off playing with that dog, and run to school. Frank will be there before you, if you do not make haste."

So John stops playing with Hero, the old dog, and does as he is bid. Now, while these children are on their way to school, I will tell you a true story of what happened to them the day of the great snow-storm.

Perhaps you are too young to remember that storm. Well, I will tell you of it. The snow fell, and fell, till it lay four feet deep on the ground. Do you know how high that is? If not, you must ask some one to show you.

Well, these four children did not come home from school; and their father, Mr. Ray, began to fear they might get lost in the snow. So he took that good dog Hero, and set out to find them.

He had not gone far when he met Frank, so tired out that he could hardly move. Frank told him that Laura and little John had got stuck in a snow-drift, and that he had come home for help while Henry had gone to a house not far off.

Then Mr. Ray felt much alarmed and went on as fast as he could, while Frank went into the house. Mr. Ray made his way through the snow, half a mile, when he met Henry and two men, who were calling loud for Laura and little John.

But these two poor children had lain down in the snow; and the snow had drifted over them, and covered them so that no one could see them or make them hear.

"Oh! what shall I do?" cried Mr. Ray, who felt very sad at the thought that Laura and John must freeze in the snow.

"I tell you what, father," said Henry: "I think that old Hero can help us. You may be sure he can scent them out, and lead us to the spot where they lie hid."

"But Hero is not here! Hero has left us in our trouble," said Mr. Ray, who felt as if he could weep with grief.

"Hark!" said one of the men. "Is not that a dog's bark?"

"Yes! that is Hero's bark! I am sure of it," said Henry. "Old Hero has found them, father. Come on! This way! This way! Hero will bring us out all right."

So Mr. Ray and Henry, and the two men, made their way through the deep snow, till they came to a place where Hero stood barking, and scratching away the snow with his feet. And, while he scratched, what should come up to sight but a little black cap?

"Here they are, father! Here's John's cap!" cried Henry; and Mr. Ray plunged into the snow, and pushed it away till he found Laura and John. There they were, but so cold that they could not speak.

The first thing Mr. Ray did was to rub them both with snow till they got warm, and could open their eyes. Then he took them home; and was not their mother glad to see them?

She put them to bed between warm blankets, and gave them some warm milk and water; and in two hours they were quite well. They will not soon forget that storm; nor will they forget the good old dog Hero, for, had he not found them out, they might have lost their lives.*

TWO AND ONE.

Two ears and only one mouth have you.
  The reason, I think, is clear:
It teaches, my child, it will not do
  To talk about all you hear.

Two eyes and only one mouth have you.
  The reason of this must be,
That you should learn that it will not do
  To talk about all you see.

Two hands and only one mouth have you.
  And it is worth while repeating,
The two are for work you must do, must do:
  The one is enough for eating.

* The occurrence actually took place at Riverdale, Mass., the 17th of January, 1867.

THE GOOSE.

This is the Goose, of her gos'lings so fond,
Who are sun'ning them-selves at the side of the pond:
When the winds blow, and when the rains fall,
Un'der her wings she will gath'er them all;
And when the sun sets, sound a-sleep they will rest
A-mong the soft feath'ers that cov'er her breast.
But when the sun rises, so fair and so red,
Then each little gosling gets up from its bed;
And off to the pond they all go with their mother,—
Each little soft gosling, each sister and brother;
And there, in the water, they swim, and have fun,
Till Jane, with some meal, comes to feed them each one.

THE BOY WITH A HOOP.

I HAVE been to school, and I got a good mark for read'ing well. I took my books home, and my moth'er told me I might go out and play in the road.

So I am here with my hoop. See! I hold my hoop in my left hand, and the stick to drive it in my right hand. Now I shall hit the hoop, and drive it on, so it will not fall.

I like to drive hoop on a cool day like this. It is now the month of March. The next month will be April, and after that will come May, and then we can find blue violets in the woods.

I love flowers; and, if you do not love them, I hope you

will learn to love them. The snow-drops are now all in bloom in our front-yard ; and my aunt has a flower she calls a daffodil. It blooms in March. The cro'cus blooms then.

At the South, where it is warm, the snow-drop was in bloom a month ago. If you never saw a snow-drop, I hope you will ask some per'son, who has one, to show it to you. It is so hardy, that you may have it in bloom while the ice is on the earth. It is white as snow.

Now I must drive my hoop. I must not stop to talk with you ; for I have not much time before dinner, and I must start for school by half-past two o'clock.

But I must tell you one thing before I go. I live in a town in the State of New York. At the school I go to, the mis'tress lets us bring the little " NURSERY " to read from. Every Tuesday and Saturday, we read in it aloud ; and we like it more than I can tell.

The mis'tress says she thinks it will be a great help to her in teach'ing us to read ; and I think so too. Shall I tell you why ? Well, be-cause we all *at-tend.* It gives us some'thing new. It is our own little magazine, made for our use, and taken by us ; and we think we ought to read it through, and read it well.

It has pieces we can learn to speak. It has pict'ures we love to look at, they are so well drawn. It does not cost much, and it gives us something fresh and beautiful every month. You must ask your teacher to take " THE NURSERY."

Now good-by. Here goes my hoop.* One, two, three, and away !

---

* The teacher should heed the difference between the sound of long *oo* as in *bloom, hoop, school, moon, soon, too,* and the sound of short *oo,* as heard in *book, took, good, wood,* &c. Many persons err in confounding the two sounds, pronouncing the *oo* in *soon,* for instance, as if it were short.

HOW THE HORSE KNEW A POOR MAN.

I will tell you a tale of a horse, whose name was "Old Jack." His master was such a good, kind man, that Jack had grown to be good and kind like him.

Jack saw that his master would not go by a poor man, but would stop and say a kind word, or give the poor man a few pence.

So when Jack saw a poor man, Jack must have thought, " Ah, here comes a poor man : my master shall not need to pull my rein ; I will stop, and then he can say a kind word at his ease."

And so Jack would stand still — so still! And he would not move till his master said, " Go on, Jack, go on." Then Jack would turn his head to look at the poor man, as much as to say, " Good-by to you — good-by ; " and then he would go on.

And, if Jack came to a part of the road where two roads met, Jack would stop ; and he would look down this road, and look down that ; and, if he saw a poor man in one of the roads, he would go that road.

And, when he came up to the poor man, Jack would stop quite still, and turn his head, and look at his master, as much as to say, " I know you like to be good and kind to the poor : see, I have found a poor man for you ; so now, if you like, you can say a kind word to this poor man."

And you may be sure that the kind word was said.

GOOD-BY, JACK FROST!

Jack Frost has left his mark on the panes of glass once more; as much as to say, "Now good-by till next winter! King Thaw is near at hand, and I must go."

What fine pict'ures Jack Frost has drawn for us on the glass! A range of hills with their white tops in the sky, and the sky all full of little stars.

A vale near by, and a lake, with ferns and fir-trees on the bank, and pearls on the ground.

A cliff, with ice on it, and a tree on the top, all white with snow; and a stream the ice holds bound, so it cannot flow.

Oh, Jack Frost! what a good pict'ure you can make! But I am not sad that you mean to leave us now.

I shall be glad to feel the soft airs of spring. I shall be glad to see the snow-drops and the early flowers. I shall be glad to hear the birds sing as they build their nests.

So, good-by, good-by, Jack Frost! Come again next winter. You are good in your turn; now you must go.

EMILY CARTER.

THE ALPHABET OF ALPHABETS.

I J K L

I   Ida is here looking at an icicle.

K   Kate is kind to the kitten in her lap.

J   Jane sees water flow into the jug.

L   Lucy looks at the sprig of lavender.

For other Letters, see pages 17, 49, 105.

A MONKEY'S TRICK.

"I will tell you of a trick I once saw a mon'key play on a poor little girl."

"If you saw it, it must be true; so let me hear it."

"Well, one day when I was at a place where there were all kinds of beasts and birds, I went near a cage which was full of monkeys.

"There was a little girl who liked to see the monkeys play their odd tricks. This little girl wore a straw hat, and the front of the hat was trimmed with some glass nuts, that looked just like real nuts.

"The little girl's name was Emma; and, after she had stood for some time a long way off, she thought it such fine fun to see the monkeys play their odd tricks that she for-got she had been told she must not go too near, and she went up quite close to the cage.

"But, as soon as she came near the cage, a great monkey put out its paw, and took hold of the glass nuts in front of her hat, and gave the hat a pull, — oh, such a hard pull!

"Poor little Emma cried out, — oh, so loud! But the monkey did not mind that. It made him give a hard'er pull still, — so hard, that the nuts came out of the hat, and poor little Emma fell down on the floor.

"Was Emma much hurt?"

"Not much; but she thought that she was, and that made her cry. But, if she was not hurt, her hat was; for it lost the glass nuts which had been put on to make it look gay, and now those nuts were in the paw of the monkey.

74

"He ran to the back of his cage, and sat on a perch, and held up the nuts in his paw, and shook the nuts with glee, and made a noise, as much as to say, 'Look at my nuts! Did you see me take these nice nuts? What a sly monkey I am to get such good nuts! Look at my nuts; but you shall not have one, — no, not one!'

" And then the monkey put a nut in his mouth.

" Crash, crash, crash, went the glass.

" The monkey jumped in fear, and spit out the glass, and made a queer face. Then he looked at the nuts, and he shook the nuts, and then he held them once more near his mouth, and then he put a nut in his mouth.

" Crash, crash, crash, went the glass once more.

" Oh, but the monkey was in a rage! He stamped with his feet, and shook the nuts, and made such a noise!

" And then he broke the nuts, and threw them from him, one by one, one by one; and, as each nut broke with a crash, oh, the monkey was in such a rage!

" It was hard not to laugh to see the monkey in such a rage; for he did stamp and jump, and shake his paw, and make such strange faces, — oh, it was an odd sight to look on!

" A good man told little Emma that he would buy her a new hat; and so she stopped cry'ing, and began to laugh with the rest, to see the monkey act so.

" But Emma should have done as she was bid. If she had done as she was bid, and had not gone so near the monkey, he could not have put out his paw on her hat, and then she would have had her glass nuts all safe."

" Ah! she should have done what she was bid. I will do as I am bid, and will not go too near the monkeys."

" Then you will be a wise, good child; for, when older folks tell you not to do a thing, they tell it for your good."

A RAIN-STORM IN MARCH.

OH, see how the wind blows and the rain falls!

I see two boys and two girls in the street.

The hat of one boy has been blown off.

See how he runs to try to get hold of it!

Do you think he will get it? Yes, by and by.

Do you see that girl there by his side?

Tell me, what does she hold in her hand?

What do you think the wind has done to it?

Ah! what a wild wind it must be to act so!

That boy who holds his cap on is wise.

He holds it so the wind cannot take it off.

He leads by the hand a girl. How it rains!

I am glad we are not out where it rains so.

THE BROKEN EGGS.

"Oh, dear me! What shall I do?"

"Why, what is the matter, little boy, that you sit on the wall, and cry?"

"Oh, dear! my mother sent me to buy six eggs. I paid for them with the ten cents she gave me. The man put them in my basket."

"Well, and what then, my little boy?"

"Why, then, as I was on my way home, I came to this stone-wall. I tried to get down from it on to the ground. But my legs are too short: I let my basket fall, and there are my eggs all broken."

"Well, my little boy, you ought to be glad you did not

break your legs as well as your eggs. I would not cry so, if I were you."

"Oh, dear! What will my mother say when she finds that the eggs are broken, and the money all gone! She will say I was a bad boy to let the eggs fall."

"I do not think she will scold you if you will run home, and tell the truth."

"Can you not give me six eggs to make up for those I let fall and broke?"

"I have no eggs to give you; but I will help you down from that wall, and then you can pick up your basket, and run home."

"I did not mean to break the eggs. Oh, dear! I did not mean to break the eggs."

"Well, do not cry. Be a little man. There! now I will help you down from the wall. Good! now here is your basket. Take it! Look! Here are two eggs not broken. That's not so bad."

"Thank you, sir: I do not think my mother will scold when I tell her the truth. I will run home, and be a good boy. Good-by, sir."

MY PET.

"Blue eyes, blue eyes, where are you going,
With your bonnet off and your hair a-blowing;
With your dress half unbuttoned, your boots not tied,
And Bruno scampering along by your side?"
"I am going to the barn, to have a good play;
To jump and to tumble and roll in the hay;

To show poor old Dobbin how to make cheeses."
"Well, mind, dear, don't tear your clothes all to pieces!"

"Blue eyes, blue eyes, where are you going,
With your satchel of books and bag of sewing;
With your neat gingham dress, and your braided hair,
And your plump, rosy cheeks, as fresh as the air?"
"I am going to school: the clock has struck eight.
Don't stop me, dear aunty, or I shall be late."
"Then run along, darling: I hope you will say
Your lessons all nicely this beautiful day."

"Blue eyes, blue eyes, where are you going,
Through the shady lane, where the men are mowing;
With your tucked pantalets and your new plaid dress?
What! you cannot tell me? you want me to guess?
Then I guess you are going, miss, out to tea;
But your sun-shade keeps hitting your hat, I see:
Well, good-by! Be as polite as you're able,
And don't, dear, eat all there is on the table!"

"Blue eyes, blue eyes, where are you going
This bright Sabbath morn, with your tresses flowing;
With your holy looks, and your steps demure,
And your dress like a snow-drift, so white and pure;
With your little clasped book, and bunch of posies, —
Buttercups, violets, lilies, and roses?"
"I am going to church, where the sweet bells call,
To ask the dear Father to bless us all!"

ELIZABETH HARRINGTON.

The

the

has a horn, and the

has a bill ; The

has a gill ; The

has a wing, that
on high it may

has a hoof, and sail ; And the

fly, or they walk,
or they soar, With

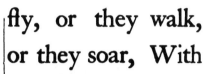

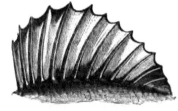

has a paw, and the

or with

has a tail; And they swim, or they or with feet, two or four.

The *Cow* has a horn, and the *Fish* has a gill;
The *Horse* has a hoof, and the *Duck* has a bill;
The *Bird* has a wing, that on high it may sail;
And the *Cat* has a paw, and the *Dog* has a tail;
And they swim, or they fly, or they walk, or they soar,
With *fin*, or with *wing*, or with feet, two or four.

DO NOT DO MEAN THINGS.

WHEN I was a small lad, I some-times used to see boys do things that I thought mean. The little boys and girls who read the Nursery, per-haps do not know what it is to be mean.

Well, some-times I used to see a big boy hide be-hind a cor'ner or a post or a box, and dart out upon a little boy to scare him when the little boy did not think any one was near.

And then the one who was scared would cry out, and say, "O John! that was mean. You had better not do that a-gain." Yes, such a trick is a mean one, and boys or girls should not do it. It is wrong; for, though no harm is meant, much harm may be done.

But there are mean'er tricks than this. Some-times I have seen boys crowd round a poor old man whom they found drunk on the ground in a back lot; and then they would stick fire crack'ers in his pock'ets, or up his sleeves, or in his shoes. And then they would fire off the crack'ers, so that they would burn the man's clothes, or scorch his face and hands.

This is a mean and wick'ed sort of fun. To get drunk is wick'ed too; but it is mean to tease a man who is too weak or sil'ly to help him-self.

The sot may have a wife or a child at home. How sad for them to see him drunk! Is not that e-nough, with-out see'ing him with his clothes burnt or torn, and all through the tricks of bad boys?

82

I have known boys to get a cat, and put the poor little trem'bling thing into a bag. And then they would call the dogs, and off they would all go to a big lot, and there the boys would let the cat out of the bag.

Then the dogs would run to catch the poor cat, and would tease it and bite it, till the poor cat would die. Was not that mean? What do you think of boys who find fun in sport like that?

I hope that no boy who reads the Nursery will ever join in a sport so wick'ed. I hope he will not play with boys who do such things. Such boys will grow up bad, hard-hearted men.

W.

Springfield, Ill.

MORNING SONG.

WITH the dawn awaking,
Lord, I sing thy praise:
Guide me to thee, making
Me to know thy ways.

All thy precepts keeping
Whole and undefiled,
Waking, Lord, or sleeping,
Let me be thy child.

MOTHER'S DARLING.

A MERRY boy,
　　Am I, you see:
I love mamma,
　　Mamma loves me.

She calls me rogue,
　　She calls me pet,
And every sweet name
　　She can get.

I laugh, I scream,
　　Sometimes I cry:
I sleep, and she
　　Sings "Hush-a-by."

I hold by chair,
　　And stand alone;
And carpet soft
　　I creep upon.

My shoes so red,
　　So beautiful,
I tug at them,—
　　I tug and pull.

Then on my back,
　　Oh, what delight
My little bare
　　Soft toes to bite!

Four teeth have I
　　As white as pearl:
What hair I have
　　Begins to curl.

I "jack-horse" call,
　　I "by-by" shake,
Play "peek-a-boo,"
　　And "clap-a-cake."

I know that doggy
　　Says "bow-wow,"
And "moo" is for
　　The moolly cow.

But once, when asked
　　By my papa
What pussy says,
　　I answered "Ba-a."

And so he thinks
I do not know
That lambs say "Ba-a,"
And roosters crow.

A merry boy
Am I, you see:
I love mamma,
And she loves me!

MRS. A. M. WELLS.

———⋅∘⋅∘⋅∘⋅———

THE ANTS.

IN March. as soon as the days get warm, we may see the ants at work. It is so strange to watch them! Each has his own place; each has his own work.

Here you may see some of the ants cutting the ground for a road, and there some of them bringing food; but it is not true that they hoard up grain for use in winter. They pass the cold days in a tor'pid state.

As I looked at them the last warm day, I would now and then see an ant try to drag a grain that was too big for him. Then four or five ants would come to help him, and share the load.

"Ah! they are odd in their ways, those ants," said an old man who stood by. "They will not let a dead ant be near them."

"What do they do, then, with the dead ants?" said I.

"Come with me," he said, "and I will show you." So he took me up the side of quite a steep place; and there, cut in the side of the hill, near the top, was a long deep trench, and in this trench lay more dead ants than I could count.

"Wait a while," said the old man, "and may-be you will see the ants bring some of the dead."

Well, I did wait; and by and by I saw some ants come slow,—oh, so slow!—and on the backs of two or three ants there was a dead ant, and it was hard work to drag their load up the hill.

But by and by they got to the top; and then they gave the dead ant a shove, and it fell into the trench with the rest of the dead; and, as soon as they saw it was safe, off they ran, and they ran down the hill, oh, so fast!—as fast as their wee legs could move.

I can tell you stranger tales than this of what the ants can do; and if you will make haste, and learn to read well, I will write more about them.

THE BEE AND THE GIRL.

THERE was a little busy bee, that flew gayly to and fro, sipping sweets from every flower.

Then a little girl who saw it said, "In some flowers there is poison, yet on all, little bee, you hover and sip."

If the little bee could only have spoken, it might have said, "Yes, I meet with poison here and there; but in each flower I find something good, and I do not touch the poison."

Let us try to find the thing that is good in those we know, and love that, while we shun their faults.

THE HUMMING-BIRD AND THE BUTTERFLY.

A FABLE.

A 🐦 met a 🦋, and, 🐝ing pleased with the beauty of its 🪶, made an offer of friend🚢. "I 🍺 🐛 think of it," was the reply : "you once 🐛 ned me." "That cannot be !" said the 🐦: "I have a great regard for you." — "Perhaps you have now," said the other ; "but when you were rude to me, 👁 was a 🐈er Ⅰ. So let me give you a piece of ad🐾: Never insult the hum🔔, as they may one day become 🏺 superiors."

KEY TO THE LITTLE PICTURES.

A humming-bird met a butterfly, and, being pleased with the beauty of its wings, made an offer of friendship. "I cannot think of it," was the reply : "you once spurned me."—"That cannot be," said the humming-bird : "I have a great regard for you." — "Perhaps you have now," said the other ; "but, when you were rude to me, I was a caterpillar. So let me give you a piece of advice : Never insult the humble, as they may one day become your superiors."

THE LITTLE BEGGAR.

I can see you, little bird,
For your chirp I plainly heard:
Tell me, did you mean to say,
" Give me some'thing this cold day " ?

That I will, and plenty too !
All these seeds I've kept for you:
Come and get them; here's a treat;
I will wait and see you eat.

Men say that you steal their wheat;
That their peas and plums you eat;
That you pick, with selfish care,
All the best ones for your share.

Oh what tales I hear of you !
Chirp, and tell me, are they true ?
Rob'bing all the sum'mer long, —
Don't you think it very wrong?

Yet you seem an hon'est bird :
(Do not fret at what I've heard ;)
Now no plums nor peas you eat;
Now you cannot steal the wheat.

So I will not try to know
What you did so long a-go:
There's your break'fast ; eat a-way;
Come and see me every day.

THE DAFFODIL.

DID you ever see a daffodil? It is a flower that blooms in March. Here is a picture of one. The leaf of a flower is called a *pet'al.* The daffodil is not the flower with the six petals spread out, but the other.

The daffodil is a pale yellow flower. The plant has green leaves, like a sword in shape, that spring from the roots. In the south of England the daffodil grows wild. The children call it the *daffa-down-dilly,* and sometimes *daffy.*

The other flower you see in the picture is called the poetic narcissus. It has six snow-white petals, spread star-like round its yellow cup, edged with bright scarlet. It has a sweet scent, and grows quite tall.

The daffodil is a bold little flower; for, like the snow-drop, it is

89

not afraid of the snow, and the cold spring winds. Here is a sweet
little poem that tells about it :—

I.

Daffy-down-dilly
    Came up in the cold
    Through the brown mould,
Although the March breezes
    Blew keen on her face,
Although the white snow
    Lay on many a place.

II.

Daffy-down-dilly
    Had heard under ground
    The sweet rushing sound
Of the streams, as they broke
    From their white winter
        chains;
Of the whistling spring winds
    And the pattering rains.

III.

" Now, then," thought Daffy,
    Deep down in her heart,
    " It's time I should start!"
So she pushed her soft leaves
    Through the hard frozen
        ground,
Quite up to the surface,
    And then she looked round.

IV.

There was snow all about her;
    Gray clouds overhead;
    The trees all looked dead.
Then how do you think
    Poor Daffy-down felt,
When the sun would not shine,
    And the ice would not melt?

V.

" Cold weather!" felt Daffy,
    Still working away :
    " The earth's hard to-day!
There's but a half inch
    Of my leaves to be seen,
And two thirds of that
    Are more yellow than
        green.

VI.

" I can't do much yet;
    But I'll do what I can :
    It's well I began;
For, unless I can manage
    To lift up my head,
The people will think
    That the Spring's herself
        dead."

VII.

So, little by little,
  She brought her leaves out,
  All clustered about;
And then her bright flowers
  Began to unfold,
Till Daffy stood robed
  In her spring green and
  gold.

VIII.

O Daffy-down-dilly,
  So brave and so true,
  Would all were like you, —
So ready for duty
  In all sorts of weather,
And loyal to courage
  And duty together!

HOW THE DOG PUT AN END TO THE LAW-SUIT.

THERE was once a strange case tried in a court of law. Two men had a dis-pute a-bout a dog. We will call one of the men Mr. White, and the other we will call Mr. Black.

"This man," said Mr. White, "stole my dog from me." Then Mr. Black said, "I did not steal his dog."

"Yes, you did," said Mr. White. "No, I did not," said Mr. Black: "I have had this dog for years."

"Days or weeks or months, it makes no odds," said Mr. White. "It is not *when* you stole my dog, but *did* you steal my dog; and I say you did. The dog I saw you walk with is my dog, and not your own."

"No, the dog is mine, not yours," said Mr. Black.

And so they went on, when the judge said, "This will not do. In this way the case will have no end; for who can tell which man is in the right? Let the dog come into court: the dog shall tell us which is the man who says what is true."

"The dog! how could the dog tell?"

"Wait, and you shall hear."

So the judge said, "Bring in the dog." And they brought the dog in. And the man who said that the dog was once his, stood back, so that the dog should not see him.

But the man who said it was his own dog, and that he did not steal it, called the dog, and the dog came and stood by him.

And when the man would say, "Lie down, sir," the dog would lie down, and do just what the man bid him do. So it was clear that the dog knew him well, and that the man must have had the dog some time.

"You see," said the man, as he looked round the court-room, — "you see how this dog does just what I bid him. Now you may know that it is my own dog, just as I said."

Then the judge made a sign to the man who said he had lost his dog; and the man came in front, and called, "Nep, Nep, Nep!"

And at the sound of that voice, which he had not heard for so long a time, the dog gave a start, — such a great start!

And he jumped up, and sprang to the man, and put his paws on the man's breast, and licked his face and his hands.

And then the dog barked, as much as to say, "Oh, my dear, dear, dear old mas'ter! are you come back? and have I found you once more? Oh! I am glad! I am glad! I am glad! What shall I do to show how glad I am?"

"You need do no more," said the judge, as he saw the dog's joy. "Now I am sure whose dog you are. Mr. White, you may take your dog home, for I am now quite sure that this bad man here did steal him from you. Good men will scorn him for the act."

Then Mr. White was glad, and the dog was glad, and all the men in the court-room — all but Mr. Black — were glad too; for they felt sure that the case had come to a good end, and that the right man had got his own dear dog once more.

"Oh! I am so glad that the right man got his own dear dog once more."

Yes, so am I. It is good to be glad when wrong is found out, and good is done. We may be sad to see bad men rob and lie, but glad to see good men get back what is their own.

THE BIRD'S NEST.

A LITTLE bird once made a nest
    Of moss and hay and hair;
And then she laid five speckled eggs,
    And covered them with care.

Five little birds were hatched in time,
    So small and bare and weak!
The father fed them every day
    With insects from his beak.

At last the little birds were fledged,
    And strong enough to fly;
And then they spread their pretty wings,
    And bade the nest good-by.

A WISE OLD HORSE.

I will tell you a true story of this horse.* He was the horse of a Mr. Lane; and Mr. Lane, on go'ing home one day, turned the horse into a field to graze.

A few days before this, the horse had been shod, but had been "pinched," as the blacksmiths call it, in the shoe'ing of one foot; that is, the shoe was so tight as to hurt the foot.

The next morning, after Mr. Lane had turned the horse into the field to graze, he missed him. "What can have be-come of old Sol?" asked he. The name of the horse was Solomon. He was so named because he was wise.

When Mr. Lane asked where old Sol was, Tim, the stable-boy, said, "I think some thief must have got him; for I cannot find Sol in the field or in the cow-yard."

"What makes you think that a thief has got him?" said Mr. Lane.

"Well, sir," said Tim, "the gate of the field has been lifted off the hinges, and left on the ground."

"That is no proof that a thief took the horse," said Mr. Lane, "I think that old Sol must have done that himself. I will tell you how we can find out. We will look at the gate; and, if there is a mark of Sol's teeth on it, we shall know he has let himself out."

So they went to the gate, and there, on the top rail, was the mark of a horse's teeth.

"Now, why should old Sol want to get out of this nice field, so full of grass and clover?" thought Mr. Lane.

* The animal belonged to the late Mr. J. Lane, of Frescombe, Gloucestershire, England; and the anecdote on which the story is founded is told by the Rev. Thomas Jackson.

94

"Perhaps," said Tim, "the blacksmith can tell·us about him."

"I will drive over to the blacksmith's shop, and see," said Mr. Lane.

So Mr. Lane drove over to the blacksmith's shop, which was a mile and a half off, and said to Mr. Clay the blacksmith, "Have you seen any thing of old Sol?"

"Why, to be sure!" said Mr. Clay. "Old Sol came here to-day, and told me I had made a bad job of it in putting the shoe on his left fore-foot."

"What do you mean, Mr. Clay?" said Mr. Lane. "A horse cannot talk."

"Oh, true! he did not say it in words; but he said it by acts as plainly as I can say it. He came to the forge where I stood; and then he held up his foot, and looked at me, as if he would like to say, if he could, 'Mr. Clay, you are getting careless in your old age. Look at that shoe. See how it pinches my foot. Is that the way to shoe a decent old horse like me? Now, are not you ashamed of yourself? Ease that shoe at once. Take it off, and put it on in a bet·ter way.'"

"Can it be that old Sol said all that by his look?" asked Mr. Lane, laughing.

"All that, and more," said Mr. Clay. "He stood still as a post while I took off the shoe. And then I put it on so it might not hurt him. And, when I had done it, he gave a merry neigh, as if to say, 'Thank you, Mr. Clay,' and off he ran. And now, if you will go back to the field, you will find him there eating his breakfast."

So Mr. Lane laughed, and bade Mr. Clay good-morning; and back to the field he drove. And there he found Tim putting up the gate; and there in the field was old Sol eating grass, and as happy as could be.

Was not Sol a wise old horse?

I must tell you one more story of him, if you will hear it.

One day a little boy, not three years old, came behind him, so close that old Sol, in kicking off the flies, might have hit him.

What did old Sol do? He lifted his hoof gently, very gently, and pushed the child away out of his reach.

THE WISE OLD HORSE.

When the maid who had care of the child came running up, she saw on its dress in front the mark of a horse-shoe.

Little boys should be careful how they go too near the legs of horses; for there are not many horses who would behave like Sol. Many horses will kick and bite.

Such horses have perhaps been treated badly. The horse knows those who are kind to him. But it is not wise to play with horses. Horse play is apt to be rough play.

EMILY CARTER.

THE SICK DOLL.

THE SICK DOLL.

"OH! can it be," said Mary, "that my doll is sick, sick, sick?
Oh! send off for the doctor, and send quick, quick, quick."
To the door came the doctor, with a rat-tat-tat:
He came with his cane, and he came with his hat, hat, hat.
He looked straight at the doll, and he shook his head, head, head:
"You must put it, ma'am," said he, "to bed, bed, bed;
You must keep it very warm, and very still, still, still;
You must give it, too, a little, little pill, pill, pill;
And to-morrow I will send to you my bill, bill, bill."

MARY'S LETTER ABOUT THE SICK DOLL.

SUCH a time as we have had with my poor Dolly! You
must know that she fell out of the window, and lay on the
cold ground all night. So the next day, when we came
home from school, Ann said, "Let us send for the doctor to
see if Rose did not take cold." *Rose* is my doll's name.

So we sent off for Doctor Charles. We did not have to
wait for him long. Soon we heard a loud, very loud knock
at the door, and Ann let him in. On his head he wore a
large hat, — too large for him, I think; and in his hand he
bore a large cane.

He did not take off his hat when he came in. I thought
this was not quite po-lite, but I did not tell him so.

"This is the sick one, is it?" said he. "Do not speak
one word, ma'am! I can tell. Now how shall I treat her, —
by the old-school practice, or the new?"

98

"I do not know what you mean, sir," said I: "you must give Rose what you think best for her."

"True!" said Doctor Charles, raising the head of his cane to his nose, and taking Dolly's wrist in his hand.

And·he looked wise — oh, so wise! — as he tried to feel her pulse.

"Ha!" said he, "fever! a high fever! The signs show that *nux* is the thing for her; and *nux*, ma'am, I shall give."

Then Doctor Charles took from his pocket a box, and from the box he took a pill, — such a small white pill! It was not so large as the head of a pin.

"Melt this in a mug of water," said he, "and give her half a tea-spoonful once an hour till the fever has left her."

"Thank you, doctor," said I: "we will do as you bid us."

He stood still, and held out his hand.

"Well, doctor," said I, "what can we do for you?"

"I want my fee, ma'am, if you please," said he.

"But I have no money about me, doctor," said I.

"No matter, then," said he: "I can send in my bill to you to-morrow."

And then the doctor left us, and Ann helped me to un-dress poor Dolly, and put her to bed. We gave her the stuff which Doctor Charles had ordered for her. Then we left her in bed, and ran off to play in the garden. When we came back, Dolly was just as well as ever, — just as well, and no better.

The next day there was a loud rap at the door, and Doctor Charles came in with his hat and cane as big as ever. "Here is my bill," said he. We looked at it. Three dollars was the charge. We thought it high, and told him so.

At last he said he would settle for a stick of candy, for he knew we had some in our bag. So we paid him the candy, and he made a low bow, and left.

UNDER THE TREE.

Two little sisters,
  Happy little sisters,
Two little sisters
  Who did well agree,
Saw a little squirrel,
  Pretty little squirrel,
Saw a little squirrel
  Under a tree.

Oh ! very softly,
  Very quick and softly,
Ran this little squirrel,
  Full of life and glee,
From a little knot-hole,
  Cozy little knot-hole,
From a little knot-hole
  Under the tree.

Then with his fore-paws,
  Tiny little fore-paws,
Then with his fore-paws
  Merrily did he
Pick up a walnut,
  Nice dainty walnut,
Pick up a walnut
  Under the tree.

And with his white teeth,
  Little shining white teeth,
Sharp little white teeth,
  As you all might see,

Did he crack the hard shell,
  Very dry and hard shell,
Did he crack the hard shell
  Under the tree.

Said Sister Fanny,
  Laughing, loving Fanny,
Said Sister Fanny
  Then to Rosalie,
" Catch the little squirrel,
  Darling little squirrel,
Catch the little squirrel
  Under the tree."

" No, no," thought Brownie,
  Cunning little Brownie,
" No, no," thought Brownie,
  " Liberty for me ! "
And among the branches,
  Crooked, leafy branches,
Up among the branches,
  Off glided he.

" Go, you silly squirrel,
  Timid little squirrel,
Go, you silly squirrel,"
  Then said Rosalie :
" If you had not run so,
  If you had not run so,
How we might have sported
  Under the tree ! "
                  CATHARINE OSBORN.

STORIES ABOUT THE SPARROW.

On a mild day last May, as I stood at the window, looking at the trees and bushes near my garden-wall, I saw two little sparrows come out from among the leaves. These birds seemed so proud and glad, that I at once said, "I think there must be a nest in that bush."

"A nest!" cried a little girl not seven years old. "Oh, please let me go and look at it! I will do no harm. Please let me go!"

What could I do but say, "Go"? And so the little girl bounded off; and soon a shout of joy told me that I was right in my guess, and that she had found a nest.

"I've found it! I've found it!" she cried. "Such a beauty, too! and five eggs in it!—blue ones, just as blue as the sky!" And there, to be sure, under a roof of green leaves, was the neatly built nest of a sparrow.

The little birds had taken any thing they could find to make their nest. Neatly woven in it were bits of red wool, which the little girl said were from what her mother had been working with. Odds and ends had got blown from the

101

window, and these the birdies had taken to make their new home look grand and gay.

The hen-bird, who had been sitting on her nest, started off when the child's hand shook the leaves near, in her search, and we feared that the fright might cause the bird to forsake her nest : but no ; for, after a short time, she flew down on to the grass, looked all around to make sure that no child was near, and then flew up, and nestled down — oh, so happy ! — down on the five blue eggs.

Days went by : many pairs of bright eyes were permitted to peep at the pretty eggs ; and once the nest came near being pulled to the ground by the plump hand of a baby-girl of two years, who was lifted up by nurse just to get one peep at the blue eggs. Baby meant no harm, — only wished to pull the nest a little nearer to herself.

At last, one bright morning, the same little girl who had first found the nest came running in with the grand news that there were five wee birdies in it ! Such funny little things, with bare bodies, and large gaping mouths !

After that, you may be sure there was not much idle time. For the parents to find food for five greedy little mouths was no easy work.

By day-light the old birds were astir, flying here, and flying there, to pick up a breakfast for their little family. Back they would come, just to pop the food into the ever ready mouths, then off again they would fly in search of more.

Truly, I think that little birds, as well as little children, should be very grateful to their parents for all the trouble they take for them.

By and by the little ones grew to be covered with feathers just like their parents ; and one day, when the little girl went to look at the nest, the little birds flew out, and soon might be seen hopping about in the garden. Being now strong enough to get over the wall, they set off to see the world.

There are many more stories I could tell you about sparrows; for, go where you will, you are pretty sure to meet with some of them.

In the Holy Land the sparrows abound, even as they did in the days when Jesus spoke of them as being sold five for a farthing, declaring that not one of them fell to the ground without the knowledge of the Father in heaven; telling his people, old and young, that the very hairs of their heads were numbered, and that surely the loving Father, who watched over the little birds, would much more take care of them, who were of more value than many sparrows.

One writer, who has spent much time in the Holy Land, tells us, that, if you were to leave your hat there out of doors a few hours, on going for it you would find that a sparrow had built her nest in it.

How would you like to be waked up in the morning by having two sparrows peck at your eyelids to make them open? "Oh, but that cannot be!" you say. Pardon me, young reader folks. An old lady, whom I used often to see, has told me of her having had for several years two sparrows so tame as to eat out of her hand, sit on her shoulder, and fly about the room.

Sometimes, when this old lady would sleep longer than usual in the morning, these little birds would fly on to her face, and peck at her eye-lids, as much as to say, "Wake up, old friend! the sun is up, and why should not you be up too? We want to be fed. We want to be petted. So, get up! get up!"

M. H.

THE BABY'S DANCE.

DANCE, little baby, dance up high;
Never mind, baby,
mother is by;
Crow and caper, ca-
per and crow:
There, little baby,
there you go,

Up to the ceiling, and down to the
ground,
Backwards and forwards, round and
round.
Then dance, little baby, and mother
will sing,
With a merry, gay carol, "Ding, ding
a ding, ding!"

M N O P

M Mary and Maud have a merry meeting.

O Off we all go within a round O.

N Nathan has in his hand a nectarine.

P Peter is playing on a pipe.

For other Letters, see pages 17, 49, 73, 137.

THE LITTLE BIRD WITH A LONG BILL.

A TRUE STORY.

HERE I am in a big arm-chair, with Katy and Mary and Jamie and Willy and Susy all round me for a nice talk; and what shall it be about? Katy says, "About that pussy-cat who could stand up on her hind paws, oh, so long, you know!" Jamie says, "About the great dog that took such good care of the old man every night. Tell us of that, auntie."

But little Susy wants to hear about the wee birdie; and Susy is such a dear pet with us all, that at last Katy and Mary and Jamie and Willy all agree to hear the story about the wee birdie. Are there any other little girls and boys who want to hear about the wee birdie? Then listen.

Once, a great many years ago, when auntie was young, she went out into the garden one morning to pick some flowers to bring in and put in pretty vases in the parlor, where she could sit with her work.

First she would pick a rose, then a pink, then a violet, and then a sprig of honey-suckle; and oh, such a large bunch as she got at last! It was so large that she could hardly hold it in her hand.

All the while that auntie was cutting the flowers, a tiny birdie, the prettiest birdie you ever saw, went with her. He had bright green feathers on the top of his head. He had wings of shining green, and a slender little brown body. But the nicest thing of all was his long bill: why, it was almost as long as his whole body! This bill he thrust into the flowers.

106

He did not stop, and stand on his feet, as other birds do; but while he was flying, and while his pretty wings were all spread, he would put his sharp long bill deep down into the sweet flowers to draw out the honey.

What was most strange was, he did not seem to fear auntie,—no, not in the least. So auntie said to herself, "Now, I will make no noise, and I will not stir quick: I will not speak, nor run, but I will walk on to the house just as slow as I can.

" I will hold these flowers so that they will not shake, and I will see if this little birdie will not follow me into the house." Was it not funny to think of walking so far with a little wild bird by one's side?

So auntie started for the gate; and down this path, and up that, she went, till she came to the gate. And all the while the birdie kept close by, with his long bill thrust into the flowers she bore in her hand. Now he would choose a rose, then a pink; but most of all he liked the honey-suckle. Do you know the honey-suckle? Well, next summer you must be sure and see one; then you can learn why the birdie liked it best.

When auntie got as far as the gate, she had a long yard to cross before she could reach the house. " Oh! will this little birdie keep on with me into the house?" she thought; and she wanted him to keep on so much! She wanted all the folks in the house to see the rare sight.

Across the yard she went,—oh! with so much care, lest she should scare the dear bird; then over the grass on tip-toe as far as the carriage road; then up a little bank over some more grass; and now she is near, very near, the door of the house.

Do you think she will get in with the bird still at her side? She held her breath, so afraid was she that the bird would fly off. But no, he was too fond of the sweet food in the flowers; and, while he flew after them, he made a humming sound with his wee wings; and that is why folks call him *the humming-bird.*

Up the steps went auntie, and into the house, for the door was open; and the bird went with her, on, on, into the room. Here she whispered,—whispered, oh, so softly, lest birdie might be scared!—whispered for the folks to come, and see the rare sight. And all the folks in the house came, and saw the rare sight.

Then what do you think the birdie did? Why, he put his little bill first into one flower, then into another, as quick as he could, as if he did not quite want to leave them; and then he put his little feet on to auntie's arm for a second, as if to say, "Thank you; now good-by." And then off he flew out of the window, and back into the garden.

I hope you will all like this story of the humming-bird as well as little Susy did.

KINGSTON, MASS.   L. N.

—◦◦◌◦◦◦—

A SHORT STORY.

A LITTLE boy, while playing the other day on a pile of wood, fell down and hurt himself. As he lay crying very bitterly, some one passing lifted him up, and said to him, "Come, my little fellow, don't cry, it will all be well tomorrow." "Well," said he, "then I will not cry to-morrow."

"Oh! do tell me some more of that good cat who saved the life of a bird. I do like that cat so much! I should like to hear another story of that cat."

"I do not know another story of that cat, but I can tell you a story of a cat who was almost as wise and good."

"Well, then, do tell me; but I *should* like to hear more of that good cat who saved the bird's life."

"Would you not like to hear of a cat who kept shop?"

"Oh, what an odd thought! But it cannot be true that a cat could keep shop."

"The story I am to tell you is a true story. A friend of mine, who wished to have some pet birds, went to a shop to buy them. When she got to the door of the shop, what should she see but a large cat who sat in the door-way!

"This cat would not stir to the right nor to the left; but there he sat, as much as to say, 'What do you come here for? I am put here to keep the door. Tell me what you want, or I shall not let you go by.'

"Then my friend said, 'I want to go into the shop, puss. I want to buy some birds. Get up, and let me come by.'

"Then the cat went to a door, and cried, 'Mew, mew;' and soon, out of a room close by, came a man, and my friend told him she wanted to buy some of his pretty live birds he kept in cages.

"So, when my friend had bought the birds, she said to the man, 'You have a fine cat there; but are you not afraid to leave him in the shop all by himself? Think of it!

He might put his claws through the wires of these cages, and kill the birds.'"

"'Why, ma'am,' said the man, 'this cat would no more kill one of these birds than you would. I call him Tom. He keeps the shop for me. If I go out of the shop, I say, "Now, Tom, you mind the birds."'

"'And does he seem to know what you want?' asked my friend. 'What if a dog or a cat should come in, and try to kill a bird?'

"The man replied, 'Tom takes his seat at the ·shop-door, just where you saw him ; and, if a dog or a cat should dare to come near the shop, Tom would spring at him at once. Tom will fight and scratch, and spit and tear, — oh, it is a sight to see! He would be a bold dog who would dare to fight twice with Tom.'

"'But what if a thief should come in, and try to steal one of the birds?' said my friend.

"'If some one comes to the door who wants me,' said the man,'then Tom gives a loud *mew*, as much as to say, "Make haste, make haste!—here is some one come to the shop?"'

"'But what if you are not near by?' asked my friend.

"'If I am not near by,' said the man, 'Tom will walk into the shop by the man's side, and will not leave him till I come in. He would not let man or boy touch a bird if I was not here to see that all was right.'

"'And will he not touch a bird himself?'

"'Touch a bird, ma'am? Tom would as soon think of eating *me*, as of eating one of my *birds*. You shall see him take care of a bird, if you like.'

"Then the man took from a cage a little young bird that could not fly, and put it on the floor of the shop. 'Tom, mind that bird,' said the man; and Tom left his seat at the door, and came and sat down by the bird.

" 'Now,' said the man, ' if I do not tell him to come away, he will stay by the side of that bird all day long, and all night, too; and no one could take the bird from him.'

" 'What a nice good cat!' said my friend, as she stroked Tom's soft, thick fur. 'Purr-r — purr-r — purr-r,' said Tom; which may have meant, 'Yes, am I not a nice, good cat? for I take care — oh, such great care — of the birds! and I would not touch a bird to harm it, — no, not if it was to save my life.'

" Then my friend put out her hand to touch the little bird that Tom was guarding; but Tom growled so that she soon drew her hand back. Was he not a nice, faithful cat?"

" Yes, I would like to see that nice, faithful cat."

"Some day we will go together to see him."

THE VIOLETS.

On the warm hill-sides, after the snow,
There do the dear little violets grow;
Hiding their modest and beautiful heads
In the dry grass, or in soft mossy beds.

Sweet as the roses, and blue as the sky,
There do they nestle, so tender and shy.
Yet their sweet secret they do not keep quite,
For their odor reveals where they hide from the sight.

FEAR NOT.

YEA, fear not, fear not, little ones :
  There is in heaven an Eye
That looks with tender yearning down
  On all the paths ye try.

'Tis he who guides the sparrow's wing,
  And guards her little brood ;
Who hears the ravens when they cry,
  And fills them all with food.

'Tis He who decks the sod with flowers,
  And pours the light abroad ;
'Tis He who numbers all your hours, —
  Your Father and your God.

Ye are the chosen of His love,
  His most peculiar care ;
And will He guide the fluttering dove,
  And fail to hear your prayer ?

Nay, fear not, fear not, little ones :
  There is in heaven an Eye
That looks with tender yearning down
  On all the paths ye try.

He'll keep you when the storm is wild,
  And when the flood is near :
Trust Him, obey Him, as a child,
  And you have nought to fear.

112

LITTLE ROSIE.

ROSIE, my posy,
  You're weary, you're dozy :
Sit upon grandmamma's knee.
  Songs will I sing you,
  Sweet sleep to bring you ;
Cuddle up cozy with me.

  I will sing ditties
  Of birds and of kitties, —
The " Song of the Well," to begin :
  How young Johnnie Stout
  Pulled pussy-cat out
When Johnnie Green let her fall in ; —

  Of timid Miss Muffit,
  Who fled from the tuffit ;
Of Bobby, who sailed on the sea ;
  Of Jack and his Gill ;
  Of the mouse at the mill ;
And baby that rocked on the tree.

  Rosie, my Rosie,
  As sweet as a posy, —
Ah ! now she is coming, I see,
  Sleepy and dozy,
  To cuddle up cozy,
And hush-a-by-baby with me.

Mrs. A. M. WELLS.

THE MAN THREATENED BY DOGS.

"How should you act if some great fierce dogs came at you as if to bite you?"

"I should take up a stone to throw at them."

"Yes, that is a good way to scare a dog off. Dogs do not like to have stones thrown at them. They are likely to run when they see you stoop to pick up a stone.

"It is thus easy to get rid of a dog without running from him.   If you run from him, he may run after you, and bark; and, if he comes up with you, he may bite.

"But, when five or six dogs come at you, there is another way to do, and that is to sit down on the ground."

"To sit down on the ground!   Why, what good could that do?"

"I only know, that, if the dogs see you seated, they will not come up to you.

"Sir Walter Scott, when he heard that not far from his gate a friend had been beset by dogs, said to him, 'You should have done what U-lys'ses did when the dogs beset him at his own gate: you should have *sat down*.   Then they would not have come at you.'

"That seems strange, but it is true.   Dogs will not harm you while you are sitting down.   It was tried by a man who had heard of what Sir Walter Scott said.

"That man re-lates, that, as soon as the dogs came near him, he sat down, and looked at them as if he did not fear them.   They stopped short a few yards off from him, and after a while sat round him, lolling out their tongues, and looking curious but calm.

"He sat still for some time, and so did the dogs.   At last he thought he might get up; but, as soon as he rose to his feet, the dogs all got up, and growled, and showed their teeth, so that he sat down once more.   They then sat down too.

"He tried this four or five times; but it was the same each time.   As soon as he would stand up, the dogs would stand up too, and threaten him.   It was plain they meant to keep him in check till their master should come, and see to him.   And so he stayed there, seated on the ground, till some one whom the dogs knew came and called them off.

" Homer, who wrote of Ulysses, and who describes him as sitting down to keep off the dogs, lived nearly three thousand years ago. So it seems that the dogs in those old times acted just as they do now. If you are ever threatened by dogs, do not forget this way of keeping them off."

———— ∙◦●◦∙ ————

HOW THE BULL LEARNED TO PUMP.

" Now, what new story have you to tell me to-day ? "

" Would you like to hear a true story of a bull ? "

" Yes, for I have not once heard a story of a bull. Was he a great strong bull ? "

" I dare say he was a strong bull, but he was not a large one. He was a small black bull, with four white legs. He lived with some cows in the field of a friend of mine ; and, when the cows came home that the girls might milk them, the bull would come with them as far as the gate, and then he would go back to the field.

" Now, in the field there was a pump, and under the mouth of the pump there was a tub to hold the water for the beasts to drink.

" One day, when the bull was in the field with the cows, he wanted some water to drink ; and he went to the pump, but there was no water for him in the tub.

" Then he cried, ' Moo-oo-oo-moo-oo-oo,' — oh, so loud ! as if he would like to say, ' I want to drink. Will no one come and pump some water for me to drink ? '

" But no one took heed of the cry, and no one came to pump water for him to drink. So by-and-by the bull must have thought to himself, 'This will not do. If no one will come and pump for me, why then I must pump for myself.'

"So the bull went up to the pump, and he put down his head till the handle of the pump rested on his horns; and then he moved the handle of the pump up and down, up and down, till the water came out with a rush, and fell into the tub, and so he got as much as he wanted to drink.

"And from that day the bull did not have to wait for any one to come and pump for him; but, when he wanted to drink, he would just walk up to the pump, and, if he did not find water in the tub, he would put his horns under the handle of the pump, and move the handle up and down till the tub would be quite full.

"But I am sorry to say that this bull, though he could learn to pump, was not kind to the cows. For when he had drunk as much water as he wanted to drink, he would stand by the tub, and would not let the cows come near, — no, not to get so much as a drop.

"When a poor cow came near, and cried quite softly, 'Moo,' as much as to say, 'Do give me just one drop of water, for I am so thirsty,' then this selfish bull would utter a loud roar, as much as to say, 'Get you gone! get you gone! I pumped this water, and no one shall have it but me.' And he would scare the poor cow so, that she would run off as fast as she could."

"Oh, what a bad, selfish bull, to take the water all for himself, and not to let the cows get one drop!"

"Yes, was he not a bad, selfish bull? But there was just one cow of whom the bull was fond; and when she came to drink, then the bull was kind, for he would act as if to say to her, in his way, 'Yes, *you* may come. Come here, and drink as much as you like; but let the rest keep far off.'

"And then the bull would pump for her, pump — pump

— pump, till she had as much to drink as she wanted; but, if more cows came near to drink at the same time, the bull would run at them, and roar out, as if he would like to say to them, 'Be gone; you shall not come here; I will not pump for such as you. Go back to your grass. Be gone. Get you off.'"

"Oh, what a shame of that bad, selfish bull to pump for that one cow, and not to let the rest of the cows have so much as a drop to drink!"

"Yes, was it not a shame? But, if the bull was not kind to the cows, he was kind to the calves; for, if a calf came up to drink, the bull would pump for her at once, and let her have as much as she wanted."

"Well, I am glad the bull was kind to the calves; but I think he might as well have been kind to the cows too, do not you?"

"Yes, I do. You must take care you do not act as the bull did, and pump only for yourself and those you love."

"I will try to take care, and to pump for all who want."

"Do: then you will be a good, kind child; for we must try to serve all, — to serve even those who are not our friends. In so doing, we shall do as the Bible bids us."

A BOY'S DUTY.

ALL good boys must every day
What their teacher says obey:
Pray and strive, and read and write,—
These make heart and spirit light;
And, with the grace of God, each can
Thus become a worthy man.

THE LADY-BIRD.

I WILL now tell you a story about a lady-bird.

You have seen the little beetle with its red, spotted wings, which every child knows as the lady-bird, — have you not?

Now, this is strange! While I am writing this page for the "Nursery" on a cold day in March, a wee little lady-bird has flown right down on my paper.

How tame it is! It comes close up to my pen. Go away, lady-bird, or I may do you harm. If you come so near my pen, it may hurt one of your legs.

"Lady-bird! Lady-bird! fly away home,
  Your house is on fire, your children alone!"

But it will not fly. It keeps round my pen as if it meant I should write none but loving words about lady-birds.

Dear little lady-bird! I would not harm you,—no, not if you made me stop writing altogether.

There! Now it flies away, but not far off. The case of its wings is marked with seven spots. There is a kind which has twenty-two spots.

In cold weather, the lady-bird loves to creep into snug corners, and keep warm. That one I look at now must have been in the house, I think, all winter.

By and by, when the roses are in bloom, what a good time it will have! Did you ever see the little green insects on the leaves of a rose-bush? Well, the lady-bird feeds on those little things, and thus does much good by freeing the leaves of the insects that spoil them.

It would be hard to find a nice rose with clean green leaves about the stem, if the little lady-bird did not fly down on to the leaf, and eat up those tiny green things that do so much harm.

In France, it is thought to be a sign of good luck to have a lady-bird light upon one's hand; and that child who should try to harm a lady-bird would be punished.

We have the lady-bird with us all the year round. It greets us in early spring, enjoys the summer with us, stays with us through the fall, and often comes out in winter to cheer us with its bright hues, and remind us that we once were young.

But I had a little story of a lady-bird to tell you. Now I think of it again, the story is somewhat sad, and I know you do not like sad stories. You would have all stories end well.

But, as you grow older, you will learn, that, if we would tell the truth, we must often tell what is sad. So I think you will hear this because it is true.

Well, a friend of mine, who writes books, once went to

see an old man; and in the old man's room what do you think he saw? He saw a cage for lady-birds.

"A cage for lady-birds! How very odd!"

Yes, was it not odd? The cage was a square glass case. It had a roof of gauze, so that the air was kept pure; and it had a floor of wet sand; and in the sand was stuck a branch from a white rose-bush, and on the leaves of the bush were ten, eleven, twelve little Lady-birds.

Now, what do you think made the old man keep that cage for lady-birds in his room? I will tell you.

Many, many years before, — when he was a young man, —he had a little daughter, whose name was Rachel; and she grew sick, — oh! quite sick, — and the folks knew she could not live.

But, just before she died, her father brought in a white rose, and gave it to her. Little Rachel took it in her thin white fingers, raised it to her faded face, and smiled.

Then her father said, "Stay, darling, give it back to me. There's a little bug on the rose. Let me push it out."

"No, no, let it stay! The dear little lady-bird!" said poor Rachel. "Let me keep it by me; and, when I want it to go, I will say, 'Lady-bird, lady-bird, fly away home!'"

"But suppose it should fly away to-day; how can my little Rachel help it?" said the father.

"Oh! I'll put it in a box, and give it nice green leaves, as many as it can eat; and I will take such care — such nice, nice care of it — that — that" —

But the poor child could say no more. She could only put the white rose on her breast, and hold her little thin fingers lovingly over it, and so fall asleep.

When she woke, it was not in this world. Rachel did not live to say, "Lady-bird, lady-bird, fly away home."

She had flown home herself,—home where she might see the face of her Father in heaven.

But over those white, thin little fingers, so still now, walked the little lady-bird, and the rose lay there on her breast.

Now you know why the old man kept a cage of little lady-birds.

EMILY CARTER. •

THE SNOWDROP.*

So many of our young friends have asked us to show them a snowdrop, that we have had this picture made for

*The botanical name, *Galanthus*, is taken from the Greek, and signifies *milk-flower*.

them. Can they tell which are the flowers of the plant, and which the leaves?

We can count six flowers in the bunch. Three of them are almost in full bloom; but the other three are not. The snowdrop is the first blossom of the year. We saw it in bloom the twentieth day of last February, and it often blooms on till April.

Is it not a dainty little flower, as it droops from its tender stalk? It has three outer petals of a pale green, and inside of these are three white ones, pure as the snow amid which it is born.

The snow and frost do not kill this brave little snowdrop. The French call it the *snow-piercer.* The Germans call it the *snow-bell;* and the old Greeks called it the *milk-flower.* It is the emblem of hope. There is a little fable which some one has made up, and which, if you care to hear, I will tell.

It is said that Hope, one winter day, stood watching the snow as it fell to the earth. Hope wished that the white flakes were fair blossoms to gladden the land, rather than snow to chill it. And then Spring, who was not far off, raised her fair arms, and, smiling sweetly, breathed on the falling flakes till they took the forms of flowers, and fell on the earth in clusters of snowdrops. On seeing this, Hope, delighted, caught one of the blossoms, and made it her emblem or sign.

MATIE AND GRUFF.

MA'TIE is my little sister: she is six years old. When she was a little baby, her mother took her to live in the country. Matie had a little black dog called Gruff. He was full of mischief.

One day, Matie left her shawl out on the piazza; and, when she went to look for it, it was gone. She searched for it a long time, and had given it up for lost, when, on going to Gruff's house, there he lay, asleep in one corner, upon that nice warm shawl! He did not like it very much, you may be sure, when we took it from under him.

Another time, Matie had a nice large paper of candy which she let fall; and then Gruff—to save her the trouble of picking it up, I suppose—put all the candy in his own mouth, not leaving one little bit for the little girl. Matie only laughed, and thought it *so* funny that a dog should like candy!

By and by we did not dare to leave any thing around; for, whenever we did so, and Gruff saw it, he would surely run off with it and hide it.

When Gruff grew to be a nice big dog, Matie used to tie him to a little wagon, and let him drag her about. But sometimes Gruff would feel like having a little fun; and then he would turn, and upset the wagon, Matie, and all!

She was not much hurt by these falls, and she would get up and laugh. But, if a boy came up as if to strike her, Gruff would bark and run at him, so that the boy would have to stop at once. Gruff liked to swim, and would go into the water, and fetch back a stick.

Gruff is not with us now; but he is not forgotten by Matie nor by any of his other friends.

MAY FOSTER.

SHIPS AT SEA.

Look at the two ships there on the wide, wide sea.
One of them is a large steam-ship, — is it not?
Yes, for it has no sails set as it moves.
What a fine breeze they must have there on the sea!
The flags fly; the waves rise and dash in foam.
The sails of one of the ships are all set.
I can see three men in a boat. Two hold oars.
Far off I can count one, two, three, four sail-boats.
I love to be on the sea when it is quite smooth.
I do not like it so well when the waves rise high.
I do not think those ships can be far from land.
If they were far from land, that boat would not be there.
Men do not go far from land in such small boats.
But the boat may be-long to the ship. Yes; it may.

UP TO MISCHIEF.

Do you see what this bad boy is doing? He has got his sister's wax doll; and he holds it before the fire that he may melt off the doll's nose, and so make fun of the doll.

Fie, sir, fie! You are too old a boy, John Blount, to find fun in such tricks. What if your sister Jane should take a sharp knife, and punch a hole in your foot-ball, and so let out all the air? How would you like that?

What if she should tear the paper off from your kite?

What if she should take your bag of marbles, and pound them all up?

She is a good girl; and she will not do such things: she will not do harm to those who do harm to her. But you would not deserve pity if she were to take your play-things, and spoil them.

That boy loves to do mischief. Can you not see it in his face? How sly he looks round at his sister!

" O John!" says she, " what are you about?"

" Giving Dolly a sweat," he replies.

" You bad, bad boy! You have spoilt that nice doll that my dear mother gave me on my birth-day. Stop!"

" Hold off, — will you?" says John, trying to keep Jane from saving the doll.

But all at once he drops the tongs and the doll, and turns pale. What is the matter? Ah! he hears a step on the stairs. It is his father's step. John did not know that his father was in the house.

Mr. Blount enters, and sees Jane trying to keep back her tears. "What is the matter?" he asks.

But Jane is no tell-tale, and she says, "Ask John."

Mr. Blount sees the tongs and the spoilt doll on the floor, and says, "So, master John, this is the kind of sport, is it, for a boy of your years? By no means will I put a stop to it. You shall have enough of it."

John looked up : he did not know what his father meant.

"Go on, sir," said his father. "Amuse yourself. I had come home to take you all, this fine day, to Bay View to dine with me. But you have chosen your sport. Now your cousin Paul shall go in your place, and you shall stay here, and have the fun you like."

If there was any thing John liked, it was to take a drive to Bay View. Now he was made to stay at home, and think of what he had done. With tears in his eyes, he saw his father and mother, his two brothers, and his sister Jane, drive off in a nice carriage to have a good time at Bay View.

"So much for finding fun in mischief!" thought John.

THOUGHTS FOR SPRING.

THE flowers appear on the earth; the time of the singing of birds is come.

Ask now the beasts, and they shall teach thee; and the fowls of the air, and they shall tell thee.

Remember now thy Creator in the days of thy youth.

He causeth the grass to grow for the cattle, and herb for the service of man: that he may bring forth food out of the earth.

Behold the fowls of the air; for they sow not, neither do they reap, nor gather into barns; yet your heavenly Father feedeth them.

Consider the lilies how they grow: they toil not, they spin not; and yet I say unto you that Solomon in all his glory was not arrayed like one of these.

Hearken unto me, O ye children! bless'ed are they that keep my ways.

I love them that love me; and those that seek me early shall find me.

Even a child is known by his doings, whether his work be pure, and whether it be right.

Bless the Lord, O my soul! and all that is within me bless his holy name!

THE KITTENS.

SEE the two kittens in the chair. One is a dark-gray kitten, and the other is black and white. See them lap milk from the dish.

The gray kitten has one foot on the rim of the dish. The black-and-white kitten has both her fore feet in the dish. She is a greedy little thing.

The old cat looks on. The old cat's fur is black and white, like the greedy kitten's. See! Kate has her left hand on the old cat's head. Mary leans on the back of the chair, and looks at the kittens.

Ruth has a spoon in her right hand, and a bowl of bread and milk in her lap. As she lifts the spoon, she stops, and looks at the black-and-white kitten. There is a ball of yarn on the floor. Can you see it?

Kate loves to see the kittens play. She has made them so tame that they will let her hold them in her lap. When she puts them on the floor, they will rush at each other as if to fight; but they do it in play.

"I'VE BEEN A-MAYING."

"I'VE BEEN A-MAYING."

THERE was a little boy whose mother used to call him Teenty. She called him Teenty because he was so small. He was not quite four years old. He lived in a small house on the edge of a wood, and not far from the railroad. His father tended a gate on the road.

Teenty had a little sister, just one year old. Her name was Grace. She was too young to go with him to pick flowers in the wood. So, early on the first of May, Teenty went off alone; and he went in such a hurry that he had one stocking off and one on, as you may see from his picture.

Poor little Teenty! It was not very warm on the first of May, and he wore no shoes. But so eager was he to go a-Maying, and to find some flowers, that he did not mind the cold wind that blew from the east.

He met a frog on his way to the wood; but it only said, "Ka-chook!" and then leaped out of his path. "You cannot scare me, Mister Frog," said Teenty. "I was not born in the woods to be scared by a frog." "Boom!" said the frog.

All at once, Teenty saw a little gray squirrel run along a stone wall and then up a tree; and Teenty spoke these lines, which he had learnt from his mother: —

> "Pretty, pretty squirrel, in the tall tree,
> Will you please to drop a nut? but crack it first for me.
> I thank you, pretty squirrel: the nut is very fine.
> Some day I'll come again, and with you I will dine."

Teenty went a little farther, and saw a bluejay, hiding an acorn in the soft wood of an old stump. "Ah, you sly bird!" said Teenty: "I know where you hide your food. You steal

130

from other birds. You tease the poor owl, and you mock the hawk. My mother says you are a rogue."*

"Queek! queek!" said the bluejay, flying up on to the limb of an oak-tree; while the crest on the top of her head rose up, and she looked like the bold, saucy bird she is.

Then she began to chatter, and make a noise, as if to scold the little boy for coming into the wood. But Teenty said to her, "Oh! you need not scold me in that way: I have as much right here as you have."

Then Teenty went on and on; and by and by the sun came out warm, and the wind changed, and blew from the south, and it was quite mild.

Teenty went on till he came to a hill in the wood; and here, in the young grass at the foot of a high rock, he found a little white star-shaped flower, nodding on its slender stem. The name of it, he did not know. On the next page, is a picture of it.

Two of the flowers are in full bloom, and one hangs its head, and its leaves are not yet spread wide. Teenty plucked his lap full of these flowers.† Then he walked home.

He felt proud that he had been a-Maying; for he had heard of the fine times which the city children have on the first of May, and he felt that he ought to show that he, too, could keep the day.

But what did his mother say when she saw him? Her first words were, "Why, you bad little Teenty! I did not know what had become of you. Where have you been?"

"I've been a-Maying," said Teenty.

---

* Teenty's mother was right in what she said of the bluejay. Wilson relates that a number of these wags of the forest will sometimes surround a poor owl, when he cannot see, and tease him almost out of his wits. They will also imitate the cry of a bird attacked by a hawk, and greatly exasperate the hawk by their mockery.

† The name of the flower is *a-nem'-o-ne*, or *wind-flower;* and this pretty name it gets from the Greek word *an'e-mos*, wind. Why it is called the wind-flower, unless because it is so easily stirred by the wind, I do not know.

And when his mother saw him with one stocking off and one stocking on, and his little lap full of flowers, and heard him say, "I've been a-Maying," she could only laugh.

WOOD ANEMONE — ANEMONE NEMOROSA.

And I think you would have laughed, too, if you could have seen this poor little Teenty, with his flowers, and his one stocking off and one stocking on.

I hope you will all be as glad as Teenty was, that May has come at last, and that the air grows more mild.

> " Sweet it is to start and say,
> On May morning, ' This is May.' "
>
> EMILY CARTER.

THE THRUSH.

"Dear little thrush, will you live with me?
I will give you a cage, and your friend I will be."

I thank you, my dear,
But I'd rather live here:
The skies they are fair,
And I love the fresh air;
The trees they are green,
And I sit, like a queen,
On a branch as it sways,
While the wind with it plays.
I have more on my table
To eat than I'm able;
For this leafy old wood
Gives me plenty of food.
But when you have said
Your lesson, and read,
Then come to this tree,
And sit down near me,
This bright after-noon,
And I'll sing you a tune.

DO AS YOU WOULD BE DONE BY.

I WILL tell you what came to pass on a cold day last March. Some boys were at play in the main street of a small town. They were rude, bad boys. All at once, they saw a young man ride by on the back of a gay horse; and, as soon as they saw him, they began to hoot, and throw snowballs at him.

This made the horse frisk, and rear up on his hind-legs. Then what did the bad boys do but hoot, and throw snowballs all the more? With jeers and loud yells, they laughed to see that the young man could not rule the gay horse.

"Go home to your mamma," cried one of the boys. "Get down from that horse, and mount a broomstick," cried another, as he threw a snowball at the young man.

What do you think was the end of all these vile jeers, and these mean acts, done to vex and plague? Why, the gay horse rose on his hind-legs so high, that he fell over backwards on the hard ice, and the young man who rode him was killed.

Then these boys, who were as cowardly as they were rude, all ran off; for they knew they had caused the young man's death, and they were afraid they should be taken up and punished.

But I am glad to say they were caught, and made to answer for their acts. The men of the town met, and said that these boys should not stay in the town if they ever again dared to insult folks in the public streets.

I hope you will not go with boys who act as these boys did. I hope you will shun them as you would shun a gang of thieves. These boys would hoot at a man if he wore gloves; or if he had on a new suit of clothes, or an old suit of clothes ; or a new hat, or an old hat ; or if he wore his hair long, or wore it short.

Young as you are, dear girls and boys who read "The Nursery," learn that you are not too young to be at heart ladies and gentlemen. Even a child is known by his doings.

Do you know what it is to be at heart a lady? what it is to be at heart a gentleman? I will tell you. It is to mind the rule which Christ lays down for us in these words: "Whatsoever ye would that men should do to you, do ye even so to them."

Ah! let us all try to live by that rule.   WM. C. GODWIN

GOOD COUNSEL.

A RHYME SIX HUNDRED YEARS OLD.

GUARD, my child, thy tongue,
That it speak no wrong :
Let no evil word pass o'er it ;
Set the watch of truth before it,
That it speak no wrong.
Guard, my child, thy tongue!

Guard, my child, thine eyes ;
Prying is not wise :
Let them look on what is right ;
From all evil turn their sight :
Prying is not wise.
Guard, my child, thine eyes !

Guard, my child, thine ear :
Wicked words will sear.
Let no evil word come in
That may cause the soul to sin :
Wicked words will sear.
Guard, my child, thine ear !

Ear and eye and tongue,
Guard while thou art young ;
For, alas ! these busy three
Can unruly members be.
Guard, while thou art young,
Ear and eyes and tongue !

HOW BUTTER IS MADE.

SEE, here is the churn with which Jane makes the nice butter we eat on our bread. First the milk is got from the cows. Then it is left to stand in a clean, cool place till cream comes on the top. Then the cream is poured into the barrel of the churn, till this is two-thirds filled; and then it is turned round and round by that handle you see, till by-and-by the nice butter comes from the shaking of the cream. This butter is taken out of the butter-milk, patted or beaten, and washed, and made up into lumps or pats, with or without salt.

Q R S T

Q Quit that quarrel about a quince.

S Susan and Sarah are singing songs.

R Robert is feeding his two little rabbits.

T These two will take tea on a T table.

For other Letters, see pages 17, 49, 73, 105, 169.

ABOUT LITTLE SAVANNAH.

THERE is a little girl whose name is Savannah, and she was two years old last Christmas. Her mamma gave her the name of Savannah because, at the time this little girl was born, her papa was with the army in the city of Savannah.

This little girl loves her papa very much. She wakes in the morning as soon as he is out of bed; and, when he gets a fire made, she calls out, "Papa, come and get your baby!"

Then he takes her up; and, when she is washed, he dresses her and combs her hair; and she is ready for play.

In winter, she sleeps in a little red flannel night-gown. As soon as it is dark, she gets this little gown, and goes to her papa, and says, "Papa, nighty on!" And, when she is ready for bed, she gives grandma and papa and mamma and brother all a kiss, and says, "Good night!"

Then she gets into her little crib; but she does not forget to take "Darling" with her. Darling is the name of her doll; and, with Darling by her side, little Savannah is soon fast asleep.

Little Savannah has a brother, who was four years old last December; and his name is Charles. He is glad he has a little sister. He loves to drag her about on his sled, and in her little wagon.

Charles has a doll that his auntie gave him a long time ago; and, though he is a boy, Charles likes it so well that he sleeps with it almost every night in his little bed close by his mamma's. He likes the doll because it is a gift from his dear aunt. Soon he will say to his sister, "You may have this doll now: I am a boy, and too old to play with dolls."

138   A WESTERN MOTHER.

"SHALL I TAKE IT?"

I have a young friend whose name is John Ray. He is not six years old. Not long ago I said to him, "John, when you want to do what you think you ought not to do, I wish you would say over to yourself these four words: '*Thou, God, seest me.*' Will you try to think of it?"

"Yes, I will try to think of it," said John.

A week after this, John came home one day hot and hungry from school. He had his slate and his satchel in his hand. In a room through which he passed, he heard the parrot, who was in a cage, cry out, "Give Polly cake! give Polly cake!"

John turned, and saw in a plate on the table what seemed to him some rolls of nice thin cake.

Now, his mother had told him never to eat cake without asking her leave; but he was now so hungry that he thought he might take a bit, and that she would not find it out.

"No one sees me," thought he.

But, just as he put his hand out to touch the cake, he thought of the words I had told him to try to think of, — "*Thou, God, seest me;*" and, as he thought of these words, John at once drew back his hand, and made up his mind he would not touch a crumb of the cake.

Then his mother came in; and, when she saw the plate, she cried out, "Oh! that careless, careless girl, to leave this poison stuff here!"

"What is the matter, mother?" asked John. "Poison stuff! Did you say poison stuff?"

"Yes. Here is some spoiled cake that Jane rolled up in

poisoned paper to use in killing flies, and here she leaves it;
and what if you or any one else had eaten a bit of it!"

"Give Polly cake," cried the parrot.

"No, Polly: it will poison you," said John's mother; and
she left the room to throw all the cake into the fire.

The next day, John came to see me; and he took my
hand, and said, "I thank you for teaching me those four
words: they have saved my life."   Anna Livingston.

HERE'S THE SWALLOW!

As I sat beneath the way-side oak,
I heard five-and-twenty little folk
Singing, " Here's the swallow! here's the swallow!
Spring is sure to follow, — sure to follow!"

I was weary, for the way was long;
But my heart leaped up to hear that song.
Vanished all at once each shade of sadness;
All my youth came back, and all its gladness.

And, in fancy, from beneath the oak,
I flew down to join the little folk,
Singing, " Here's the swallow! here's the swallow!
Spring is sure to follow, — sure to follow!"

There are some kinds of birds that do not live in the
North all the year round. When the winter comes, they fly
far, far away to the South; but by and by, as the spring
comes on, these birds come back to us.

The swallow is one of these birds. It does not come back to us till April or May. When we see it, we may know that the warm, bright days of spring are close at hand.

Few birds fly so fast as the swallows. They can fly seventy or eighty miles an hour. They seem never tired, but dart about, now here, and now there, after the insects on which they feed.

When these birds fly far off to the South, they do not forget the place where they have once built their nest. They are almost sure, the next spring, to come back to the same place, and to make use of the same nest.

I will tell you a true story of some swallows. Of all places in the world, where do you think these swallows built their nest? I know you cannot guess; so I will tell you: they built their nest in a school-room.

"In a school-room? But did not the boys and girls scare them off?"

No: for they were good and kind boys and girls; and they said to one another, "Now, we will treat these birds well. We will not tease them nor harm them in any way; and we will see if they will not stay."

Well, the swallows did stay; and they built their nest up against one of the timbers of the roof. They hatched their eggs, and reared their young, and taught them to fly in the room.

"What! did they fly in the room when the girls and boys were saying their lessons?"

Yes: these good children mind'ed their lessons all the same; but they took care to have the window open all the time, so that the swallows could fly out and in when they wanted to.

Well, when the cold weather came on, these swallows left their nests, and flew far off to the South. But, the next spring, back they came to the school-room. But the day was cold, and the window was shut.

Then what did these swallows do but fly against the glass, as if to say to the children, "Let us in! Let us in! Here we are, come back! How do you all do? Let us in to see if our old nests are still left."

The children opened the window, and the swallows flew in; but, when they found the old nest was not there, they flew out, and brought back clay in their beaks, and built a second nest in the same place.

The children would say their lessons, and sing their songs, while the swallows flew in and out; and the hen-swallow would sit on her nest, while the male would perch on a shelf near by, and twitter, as if to say, "We feel quite safe here among these kind children."

Always be kind. Even little un-tamed birds, you see, will show that they do not for-get kindness. Do not need'less-ly destroy a nest or any little bird.

David tells us (Psl. lxxxiv. 3) that swallows were allowed to build their nests even in the temple; and Jesus said of sparrows, "One of them shall not fall on the ground without your Father." Matt. x. 29.*

There are men and boys who seem to think that birds and beasts have no rights because they cannot help themselves when we choose to kill them. But the truly brave and good child will be all the more' tender to birds or beasts because they are in his power.

The horse is too often badly treated, and made to bear too heavy loads; and the beasts that are killed for food are made to suffer much more than is right. I hope the young readers of "The Nursery" will be kind to all. Uncle Charles.

* Some children have a bad habit of pronouncing *swa'llow, fol'low, spar'row,* &c., as if they were spelt *swaller,* &c. Give to *ow* the full sound of long *o* in *go*.

SPRING IS HERE.

THE BIRDS.

CHILDREN, this is May :
Come forth all to play !
Hear the young birds sing !
Hear them hail the spring !

Sparrow, robin, linnet, thrush, —
How their merry notes out-
gush !
By their songs they seem to
say,
" Thanks, oh thanks, for life to-
day ! "

Children dear, shall we not be
Grateful as the birds we see ?
Come, oh come, from far and
near !
Come, and sing, " Spring, spring
is here ! "

144

Come, and pluck the daisies ;
Come, and sing their praises.
Pluck the violets blue, —
Ah ! pluck not a few.

God giveth all : oh, learn it in your
childhood !
Worship Him at your tasks, with
fond endeavor ;
Worship Him at your sports ;
worship Him ever ;
Worship Him in the wildwood ;
Worship Him amid the flowers ;
Worship Him at all hours.

Thank Him for duty,
And thank Him for all beauty, —
For the music of the birds,
For the grass, and for the herds.
Pluck the buttercups, and raise
Your voices in His praise.

EDWARD YOUL, (Altered).

THE DAISY.

THE MOUSE THAT CAN SING.

"A FRIEND of mine has a mouse that can sing."

"A mouse that can sing! Oh! but is that true?"

"Yes, it is true; and I have heard of other mice who could do the same. When it is quite still at night, and there is no noise in the room, then my friend hears a low 'scratch, scratch, scratch;' and out from a hole in the wall comes a nice gray mouse.

"This mouse will look first this way, and then that; and when he sees that there is no cat near, and that no one will hurt him, then he sits, and sings a sweet song.

"My friend says that no song of a bird can be more sweet and clear. And, when this dear little mouse has sung his song, he will look round with his bright black eyes, as much as to say, 'Good night,— good night to you all.'

"And then he will run back to his hole, and you will hear his song no more that night. But he will not let any one come near him to touch him; and, if any one comes near, he will run to his hole, and then he will not sing at all."

"Oh, I hope the cat will not catch that good mouse!"

"So do I. I should not like to have the cat catch that good mouse. That would put a sad end to his sweet song."*

* Instances of singing mice have been not unfrequently recorded. Of the sensitiveness of the mouse to musical sounds, we have had many examples.

HOW FRISK CAME HOME.

ONE of my friends had more dogs than she knew what to do with: so she thought, "I will give one of my dogs to my aunt in Troy, for I think she will like to have such a nice black-and-white dog as Frisk."

So Frisk went to his new home, twenty miles off.

But Frisk did not like his new home so well as his old one. In his old home, he was a great pet: but, in his new home, no one did care much for Frisk; and they put a chain on his neck, and tied him up in the yard.

So Frisk sat in the yard, and tried to get rid of his chain. But this he could not do. Then he was quite sad; and he thought, "Oh! if I could but get back to my old home,—if I could but get back to my old friends once more!"

But Frisk did not know the way back to his old home: for, when they sent him to his new home, they had put him in a bag; and they had tied up the top of the bag, so that Frisk might not see the way they took him. So Frisk was sad be-cause he was tied by a chain, and because he did not know the way back to his old home.

But it is said, "Where there is a will, there is a way;" and so Frisk found it, as you shall learn.

One day, when the man took Frisk out in the road for a run, Frisk thought to himself, "This man does not like me much, for he will chain me up if I let him take me back to my new home. So I will take a run all by my-self, and not with the man."

And then Frisk ran under a bush, and sat there till the man was far off; and when the man turned round, and did

146

not see Frisk at his heels, the man called out, "Frisk! Frisk! Here, sir, here! Good dog! Here, Frisk! Frisk! Frisk!"

"No: I will not come; I will stay here and hide," thought Frisk. "You may call me *good dog*, but I will not come. I try to be a good dog, and yet you chain me up."

Then the man thought he should find Frisk at home; but, when the man got home, no Frisk was to be seen. The night came, and still no Frisk was to be seen.

"I think Frisk must be dead," said the man.

"But was Frisk dead?"

Wait, and you shall hear. A whole week went by, and nothing was seen or heard of poor Frisk.

But one day when my friend, with whom Frisk had first lived, went out with her children, Mary and Edgar, to walk, they saw, a short way from the house, a poor, thin black-and-white dog by the road-side.

He was quite lame; for his feet had been cut with sharp stones, and his hair was red with blood.

Then all at once Edgar cried out, "O mother! look! look! look if that is not our own poor Frisk come back to his old home!"

"So it is our own poor Frisk," said my friend. "But how could he have found his way back twenty miles, all the way from Troy to this place? For he was tied up in a bag when we sent him off. Poor Frisk! How thin and ill you look!"

Then Edgar went up to Frisk; and the poor dog did not well know what to do, so glad he was to see the little boy. And my friend went up, and Mary went up, and they all patted Frisk on the head.

Then they took Frisk home, and gave him nice milk and good meat; for he had not had food for whole days. He was glad to be fed; but he was still more glad to be in his old home, and to see my friend and her children once more.

As soon as he was strong enough to do it, he jumped and barked for joy; and he tried to lick the hands and face of my friend, as much as to say, " I am so glad to be at home once more!   Oh, let me stay! pray, let me stay!"

"And did your friend let Frisk stay at home?"

Oh, yes! my friend let him stay; and Frisk is a large dog now, and he has not left his dear home more. You may see the picture of Edgar and Mary trying to make Frisk look

at the letters in " The Nursery;" for my friend takes " The Nursery," and says she likes to read it as well as the children do.

THE LITTLE GRAY MOUSE.

LITTLE gray mouse, little gray mouse,
I beg you to stay in your snug little house:
If you come out here to eat but a crumb,
The old cat will kill you, as sure as you come.
Little gray mouse, little gray mouse,
I beg you to stay in your snug little house.

THE FROG AND THE CAT.

As the spring season comes on, you may hear the frogs croaking in the ponds and low wet places. The croak of the frogs is to me a pleas'ant sound, for it is a sign of pleasant weather. Almost always, when you hear the frogs croak at sundown, the next day will be fair and mild.

If you were to ask the frog where he would like to live, and if he could speak, what do you think he would say? Why, he would say, "Oh! let me stay here by this pond, where the ground is nice and wet; for I am always so thirsty, I like to have plenty to drink."

And if you did not mind the wish of the frog, but took him off to a place where there was no water, and where the ground was dry, the frog would soon grow thin and die; for he not only drinks with his mouth, but he sucks up water like a sponge through little holes in his skin.

A friend of mine once caught six frogs, which he kept in a bowl of water. As long as there was plenty of water in the bowl, they looked fat and well; but, if my friend took them out when the day was hot, they soon grew thin and ill.

These frogs be-came quite tame,—so tame that they would take their food from my friend's hand. They were fond of flies, and could catch them quite fast, and so my friend put them to some use; and how do you think he did it? I will tell you. When the fruit was laid out on the side-board, my friend used to place these frogs round it to act as guards; and they kept off the flies so well that not a ripe plum or peach did the flies touch.

I must tell you one queer thing about frogs. After the frog has worn his skin for some time, and thinks it is getting either very tight or very shabby, he makes up his mind to get rid of it; for he knows there is a nice new skin underneath it.

So he finds out five or six other frogs who, like him, have made up their minds to change their skins. Then two of these frogs take hold of the one whose coat is to come off. These two hold him tight round the waist, while one or two other frogs give little bites and pulls at his skin; and so, by and by, first one leg, and then the other, and at last the whole body, is set free from the old skin; and then the little frog appears in a fresh skin, of which he must be quite proud; for he croaks away, as if he wanted all the folks to come and admire his nice span-new coat.

I have told you that frogs are quite thirsty, and like to live in damp places; but I must not forget to tell you that I know of one frog who in this was not like all the other frogs I have heard of.

His name was Bob. He had made his way, through a hole in the wall of the kitchen, into the house of a friend of mine. For some time Bob was shy; but at last, seeing that all the folks were good to him, he got quite tame, and would come out to be fed.

He would sit on the kitchen hearth for hours in winter; so that Bob and the old white cat grew to be great friends. When it was cold, Bob would nestle down under the cat's fur; and the cat would do him no harm, but seem to like to have him near.

Once this little frog hopped into a room where there was a monkey; and, before Bob could jump out of the way, the monkey seized him. Bob thought his last hour had come: but he kicked so that the monkey let him drop; and off Bob hopped into the kitchen to his dear friend, the old white cat, who gave him a nice place by her side on the hearth.* You may see them both in the picture.

"Could I tame a frog so he would act like Bob?"

I do not know of another frog who would stay in the house like Bob. He was an odd frog, and I think you would find it hard to match him.

"I have seen boys throw stones at frogs."

I hope you will never be so foolish and cruel as to throw stones at frogs. The frog is one of the most harmless of animals.

AUNT KATE.

---

* The *ea* in *hearth* has the sound of *ea* in *heart*, not of *ea* in *earth*.

"THE NURSERY HAS COME."

Children. — Look, papa! "The Nursery" has come!

Edwin. — The postman has just left it at the door.

Mary. — Mine has come, too, papa.

Tommy. — I want to see the pictures. Show me the pictures. Let me see the man and the dogs.

Ruth. — Read me one of the nice stories.

152

Papa. — If you all speak at once, little ones, how shall I know what you say?

Edwin. — I say, papa, "The Nursery" has come.

Papa. — Is that what the bells are ringing for?

Ruth. — No, papa, the bells are ringing for one o'clock.

Tommy. — I want to see "The Sick Doll."

Mary. — Be good, Tommy, and you shall see my copy.

Papa. — Now, before you begin to read your little magazine, you must cut open the leaves carefully and neatly.

Mary. — Mine are all nicely cut.

Edwin. — I know a boy who cuts open the leaves with his fore-finger.

Papa. — That is a slovenly way of doing it. I hope you never spoil the pages in that way.

Edwin. — No, sir: I have a little paper-cutter I made of wood. I scraped the blade sharp with glass.

Mary. — And I have an ivory knife.

Papa. — Learn to take good care of your books. By and by you shall have the numbers of "The Nursery" bound up in a volume; and a very pretty volume they will make, I think. You must try not to soil the leaves.

Edwin. — I mean to try to keep my numbers as long as I live. I have read them through three times.

Mary. — So do I mean to try to keep mine.

Ruth. — Mayn't I play that my doll is sick?

Edwin. — Yes; and I will be the doctor.

Mary. — And I will be the nurse.

Tommy. — What shall I be, papa?

Papa. — You, Tommy, shall be the boy who holds the doctor's horse. Here he is at my feet. Take him out.

Edwin. — Be gentle with him, Tommy.

Papa. — Now run, little ones, and read the nice stories. Leave me to my work.

THE TWO WHITE CATS.

Now listen to me while a story I tell
    Of two snow-white pussies who lived in a tree,
And who knew, without hearing a clock or a bell,
    The right time to come for their breakfast and tea.

They would run, bright and early, across the wet grass,
    And stand on their hind-feet, or scratch with their fore ;
Or, with little white paws, softly tap at the glass ;
    Or come, and cry "Mew," both at once at the door.

They would flatten their noses against the cold pane,
    When they saw on the table the toast and the fish;
Crying, "Mew! mew!" which meant, "Oh! do give us a grain
    Of the cream in that cup, and the meat in that dish."

In the room which they spied through the window, there sat
    A good little girl — but her name I can't tell :
When she saw looking at her each poor little cat,
    Though she could not help laughing, she treated them well.

First, a saucer of milk she set down on the mat.
    "Mew! mew!" cried the cats, when they knew what was in it.
Then she opened the door ; and they came pit-a-pat,
    And their whiskers they dipped in the milk in a minute.

The little girl laughed as each quick little tongue
    Went " lip-lap " and " lip-lap," and so got the milk ;
And soon a loud " purr " both together began,
    As she stroked their white fur with a hand soft as silk.

And, after their breakfast, she begged they might stay
  For one little half-hour, just to sleep on the rug;
For out·in the cold they had long been away,
  And both did so long to lie down warm and snug.

And now, little children, my story is told ·
  Of the two snow-white pussies who lived in a tree;
Who knew when to come, through the frost and the cold,
  To beg at the door for their breakfast and tea.

                                   GERDA FAY.

THE TWO MEN AND THE BEAR.

Two men were once going through a thick wood.

"I fear," said one, "that we may meet with wild beasts: I see the tracks of their paws on the ground."

"Fear not, friend Wise," cried the other, whose name was Brag. "Should a wild beast come up to us, we will stand by each other like men. I have a strong arm, a stout heart, and do not know what fear is."

"Hark!" cried the first, as a low growl was heard from a bush close by. Quick as a flash, Brag, who was light and spry, climbed up a tree, and left his friend Wise, who was not so spry, to face the wild beast alone.

But Wise was quick to think what to do. He could not fight; he could not fly; so he laid himself flat on the ground, and held his breath so as to seem quite dead.

Out of the bush rushed a great black bear. The beast ran up to poor Wise; while Brag, sick with fear, looked down from his perch in the tree.

The bear put his nose down, and snuffed all around poor

Wise, from his ears to his toes. But Wise held his breath all the while, and did not wince or move; and at last the bear, thinking he must be dead, walked off without doing him any harm.

When Brag saw that the bear had gone, he came down from the tree. He felt some shame at having acted so like a coward; but he thought to pass it off as a joke.

"Well, friend Wise," said he, "what did the bear say to you when he had his mouth down at your ear?"

"If he could have spoken," said Wise, "I think he would have said that I was a fool to trust a boaster like you."

Do not boast, but act.

GOING TO SLEEP.

The sun has gone down, and the birds are asleep,
And so are the cows and the pretty white sheep:
The nursery is quiet, the toys on the shelf,
And Freddy is left in his cot by himself.

And is he afraid in the dark? Not at all.
He feels very sure there are friends within call.
Besides, he forgets not to whisper his prayer
To God for forgiveness and comfort and care.

So down on his pillow he nestles his head,
And settles himself in his warm little bed;
And, grateful and happy, to sleep Freddy goes:
He will wake up to-morrow as fresh as a rose.

THE BLIND MAN LED BY A DOG.

As I went through the street last week, I saw a poor blind man led by a dog. The blind man held a string, which was tied to the dog's neck, so that the dog could guide him, and lead him out of the way of the folks they met.

It was a warm day, and the poor dog felt as if he should die from thirst; so he tried to stop, and drink the foul water that lay on the ground. But the blind man, who did not know that the dog felt as if he should die from thirst, tried to pull him away by the string.

Then the dog made a low, sad cry, as if he was in pain; and two kind boys, who stood near, went up to the blind man, and said, "Your dog wants water, sir. If you will let us lead him to a shop close by, we will give him some good clear water to drink."

The blind man said, "I thank you. I shall be glad if you will lead my poor little dog where he can get some good

157

clear water to drink. I will wait here till you bring him back."

On the coat of the blind man, in front, was a paper with printed words on it. It told how he was "*totally blind;*" that he had been a fireman, and had lost his sight at a fire.

The boys stopped to read this paper and to ask some questions. But the poor little dog was so very thirsty that he kept pulling at the string to get at the water which lay in the gutter of the street.

Then the boys led the dog to the shop; and a kind man who kept the shop filled a pail with fresh, cool water, and gave it to the dog to drink. Oh! how glad the little dog was to get the fresh, cool water!

Then the man who kept the shop gave the dog some meat to eat, and said to the boys, "Go tell the blind man to come in here, and I will give him a slice of cold beef and a cup of tea."

So the boys told the blind man, and he came in and had a good meal. Then he thanked the shop-man and the two boys for their kind acts. Then he took the dog's string and said, "Come, little dog," and so went off up the street.

IDA FAY.

THE SELFISH BOY.

LEARN wisdom from Barnaby Pelf:
All he got he would keep for himself.
    A pie or a cake
    He would greedily take,
And hide in his box, on a shelf.

To friends, he would never cry, "See!
Come share this nice morsel with me;"
    But, with greed in his face,
    He would sneak to some place,
Where alone with his food he could be.

Was he happy with all that he got?
Very sure you may be, he was not.
    Who freely do give
    Alone truly live:
Of the selfish man sad is the lot.

"O Barnaby, Barnaby, dear!"
His mother would say, with a tear,
    "If so selfish you grow,
    None will love you, I know:
To be loved, we must *love;* that is clear."

One day he had eaten his fill,
When he grew all at once very ill:
    They thought he would die,
    So sick did he lie,
So pale did he grow, and so chill.

Then he prayed as he lay in his bed;
And, when he got better, he said,
    "I am healed, they shall find,
    Both in body and mind:
I live, but the glutton is dead."

But, when he got well, did he still
Do all that he promised when ill?
    I am happy to say,
    Not in vain did he pray:
He is changed both in heart and in will.

Now Barnaby tries all he can
To be a good, liberal man:
    To the needy he gives,
    Well and happy he lives;
And I hope you will choose his new plan.

EMILY CARTER.

THE DOLL'S HOUSE.

161

THE DOLL'S HOUSE.

THERE were once two little dolls; and the name of one was Pet, and the name of the other was Pink. Pet, who was Alice's doll, had a house all to herself. Pink, who was Rachel's doll, had no house, but only a little cradle which Rachel's brother had made with his pen-knife out of a piece of wood.

One day Rachel went to see Alice, and Alice showed her Pet's little house. It was a nice little house; and, if you will look at the picture of it, you will see that it had all the things a rich doll could wish.

In the four rooms of the little house were a sofa, a table, a clock, chairs, a wash-stand, a basin and pitcher, a grate for fire, a pair of bellows, and I know not how many more things, good both for use and show. I hope my little readers will find them all out from the picture.

Rachel spent half an hour looking at all the nice things, and admiring them; and, when she was ready to go home, she gave Alice a kiss, and said, " I thank you for showing me your doll's house. If you will come and see me at my home, I will show you my doll's cradle. Then I will take you into my garden, and show you a rose-bush all in bloom."

"I think I shall like the rose-bush quite as well as you like my doll's house," said Alice.

"Oh! but a rose-bush is not so rare a thing as a doll's house like this," re-plied Rachel. "We can see roses every day in June, but not a house like this. What a nice little kitchen! I can see a sauce-pan, a dust-pan, a tea-kettle, a gridiron, plates on shelves, a table, and I know not how many more things. How nice and bright you keep them!"

Alice held Rachel by the hand, and said, "Would you like a doll's house just like mine?"

"Oh! I would like it so much!" replied Rachel. "But I can come and see yours, and that makes me almost as glad as if I had one of my own."

"You shall have one of your own," said Alice. "You shall have mine."

"Oh, no! you do not mean it," said Rachel.

"Yes," said Alice: "my father said to me last week, 'Alice, you are now old enough to give up playing with dolls. You may give away your doll-house.'—'May I give it to whom I please?' asked I. 'Yes,' said my father. 'Then I know to whom I will give it,' said I. You, Rachel, are the little girl! The doll-house is yours; and Pet is yours. She will be good company for Pink."

Little Rachel did not know whether to cry or to laugh. At last she threw her arms round Alice's neck, and kissed her; and I think there was just one little tear on Rachel's cheek as she gave the kiss.

IDA FAY.

EDDY'S BIRTH-DAY PLAN.

I'M six years old this very day;
Three feet, nine inches high;
Full six and forty pounds I weigh:
I'm quite too big to cry.

I'm very sure my mother dear
Will like my birth-day plan;
Which is, through all my seventh year,
To try to be a man.

ST. LOUIS.

A HARD DAY'S WASH.

Bertha is eight years old, and Mary is five. Bertha has two dolls, named Ada and Rose; and Mary has two, named Jane and Sophy. These little girls have nice times together, playing with their dolls. They dress and undress them, take them to walk and to ride, put them to bed, and one day they washed all their clothes.

I must tell you about this famous washing-day. Bridget, the chambermaid, had been washing some towels, and had left a tub of warm suds standing in the wash-room. Bertha spied it.

"Now, Mary," said she, "I tell you what: we must have a wash. My Ada has no clean stockings, and your Jane's dress is not fit to be seen. Let us go and wash our children's clothes, as good mothers ought to do."

"Oh, yes!" said Mary: "what fun it will be! But we must ask mamma first."

Mamma thought they would slop themselves all over, and that they had much better make-believe wash in their little baby-house tubs. But they had set their hearts on having a

HANGING OUT THE CLOTHES.

wash with real water; and so mamma, "just for this once," let them have their way.

Then what a getting together of clothes there was! Poor Ada was left lying on the floor, without a rag upon her (I hope she did not take cold); Jane had to keep herself warm in her night-gown; and Dot, the rag-baby, was put to bed.

As soon as the clothes were in the tub, Bertha went through the form of rolling up her sleeves over her bare arms. Then she plunged her hands into the suds, and went to work with a will.

"Dear me!" said she: "what a job it is to wash for such a large family!"

"Yes," said Mary, as she poured in more water from her little mug: "children don't know how hard we mothers have to work; do they, Bertha?"

"Your Jane's dress is covered with grease-spots," said Bertha. "I shall teach my children to be more careful of their clothes."

Such a rubbing and such a splashing as they kept up! And such rich suds as they made! I doubt if clothes were ever washed so clean before. After being washed, of course they had to be wrung out, which was another great piece of work.

Then they put the clean linen into a basket, and took it into the play-room, where Bertha put up a piece of twine between the wall and a chair for a clothes-line.

While this was going on, Mary said she thought children ought to learn to be useful, and that she meant to teach her doll Sophy to wash. So Sophy was seated down at a tub on the floor, and then Bertha and Mary hung out the linen to dry.

After they had hung out all the dolls' clothing, Bertha said they might as well put up some of their own things with the rest of the clothes-pins. So they kept on hanging out until the line would hold no more; and even then they could hardly make up their minds to stop work,

When the nurse put them to bed that night, they both said they were very tired; and the nurse said she should think they well might be after such a hard day's wash.

THE BOY WHO WORE OLD CLOTHES.

A NEW DIALOGUE FOR PRIMARY SCHOOLS.

ARTHUR RICH.

YOUR hat is too big for your head, Martin Lee;
　Your jacket is thread'bare and old;
There's a hole in your shoe, and a patch on your knee, —
　Yet you seem very cheer'ful and bold.

MARTIN LEE.

Why not, Arthur Rich?　For my les'son I say,
　And my du'ty I try hard to do:
I have plen'ty of work; I have time, too, to play;
　I have health; and my joys are not few.

ARTHUR RICH.

See my cap, and my boots, Martin Lee, how they shine!
　My jack'et, my trow'sers, — all new!
Now, would you not like such a nice rig as mine?
　Come, give me the an'swer that's true.

MARTIN LEE.

Such clothes, Arthur Rich, would be-come me and please;
　But I am con-tent in the thought
That my mother is poor: so I'd rath'er wear these,
　Than have her work more than she ought.

ARTHUR RICH.

You are right, Martin Lee, and your way is the best;
　Your hat is now hand'some to me:
I look at the heart beat'ing under your vest,
　And the patch'es no longer I see.　EMILY CARTER.

THE ALPHABET OF ALPHABETS.

U V W X Y Z

U   Under the umbrella here we sit.

W   We are here waiting for William.

V   Virginia is viewing a vessel out at sea.

X   Exactly at six I expect him.

Y   Young Sydney asks you Why?

Z   Zachary shows a cut of a zany.

For other Letters, see pages 17, 49, 73, 105, 137.

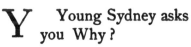

a b c d e f g h i

j k l m n o p q

r s t u v w x y z

SUSAN AND BUNNY.

I will tell you a true story about a little girl and her tame squirrel. The name of the little girl is Susan, and the name of her squirrel is Bunny. Soon after Bunny was born, and before his eyes were open, Susan's brother found him in the woods, and gave him to Susan to keep.

Susan fed him, and made a soft, nice bed for him to sleep in; and Bunny grew very fast. In a few days he opened his eyes; but Susan soon found that he could not see: poor little Bunny was blind!

Susan now grew very fond of him, and he knew her from any other person. When she came into the room, she would call, "Bunny! Bunny!" and then Bunny would try to come to her. But, instead of coming to her, he would run round and round in a ring, and would not get any nearer to his friend. This was because he could not see.

And, when Bunny found he was not any nearer to his friend, he would stop running, and try to listen; but sometimes he had run round and round so much that his head would be dizzy, so that at first he could not keep it still.

Then Susan would call Bunny again, and would drum on the floor. He would listen; and then he would come nearer and nearer to the sound, until he would find himself in his friend's hands. How glad he would be when he found himself in his friend's hands!

Susan would pat his head, and stroke his soft fur, and tell him what a good, dear Bunny he was; and then she would give him a nut to eat. Bunny would take the nut, and run up on

170

Susan's shoulder, and there break the nut open with his sharp teeth, and eat the meat that he found in it.

When he had eaten the meat, he would run down Susan's arm, and smell of her hands, and try to find out whether she did not have one more nut for him. If Susan had one more nut shut up in her hand, Bunny would try to put his nose between her 'fingers, and get at the nut.

Then Susan would give him one more nut, and another after that, till he had eaten all he wanted. If there were any nuts given to him that he did not want to eat at the time, he would hide them away in his little house; and there he would seek them when he was hungry, and no Susan was by to feed him.

One day last week, Susan came home from school, and went to see her dear Bunny. She called him, and called him, but he did not come at her call; and she could not find him, look for him where she might. He had gone out of his little house, and had strayed away, no one could tell where.

Perhaps a dog or a cat had killed him. Perhaps he had run out on the fresh spring grass, and could not find his way back; and perhaps he would starve, for how could he see to pick up a nut? The tears would start in Susan's eyes at these thoughts.

Two days went by; and on the third, as Susan was hunting for her little blind squirrel among the hemlock trees, she heard a little "Squeak! squeak!" and looking round on the low branches, she saw poor little Bunny.

She ran and took him up; and oh how very glad he was when he found he was in the hands of his own dear friend! Susan was glad too. Bunny was almost starved; but Susan fed him, and gave him some nice milk: and now poor little blind Bunny is quite well once more, and happy as a king.

H. H. D.

THE CAPTIVE BUTTERFLY.

POOR little butterfly under the glass,
You want to be out, flitting over the grass;
You want to be out on your favorite flowers,
To sip their sweet honey, these warm summer hours.
In prison no longer I'll keep you; and so,
　　Butterfly, go! butterfly, go!
　　Butterfly, butterfly, butterfly, go!

Your wings are so beautiful, now they are spread!
How bright are their colors,—brown, yellow, and red!
Go fly to the rose, and alight there, and sip
The dew off its leaf with your little wee lip;
Go rest there, and rock while the June breezes blow.
　　Butterfly, go! butterfly, go!
　　Butterfly, butterfly, butterfly, go!

Your life is so short that it shall not be said
I made it unhappy before it had fled.
Go roam in the garden, go follow the bee,
Go flit in the sunshine, enjoy all you see.
In me, little thing, fear never a foe.
　　Butterfly, go! butterfly, go!
　　Butterfly, butterfly, butterfly, go!

EMILY CARTER.

KEEPING SHOP.

Mary. — Good morning, Mrs. Spinage.

Bertha. — How do you do, Mrs. Primrose? What can I sell you to-day?

Mary. — Have you any white sugar?

Bertha. — Yes, ma'am; the best of sugar. Taste it. Give that sweet little baby a lump. How much will you have?

Mary. — Five pounds; and here is a basket to put it in.

Bertha. — Yes, ma'am. It will come to two dollars. Any thing else?

Mary. — Have you any snuff?

Bertha. — No, ma'am; but we have onions.

Mary. — Do you keep peppermints?

Bertha. — No, ma'am; but we have very nice potatoes.

Mary. — I must find a dry-goods shop, for I wish to buy a hoop-skirt for baby.

Bertha. — Yes, ma'am; you'll find one just round the corner.

Mary. — Good-by, Mrs. Spinage. I may call again.

Bertha. — Do, ma'am. You've dropped your sun-shade. Don't forget that, for you need it with such a small bonnet. Good-by, Mrs. Primrose.

THE HEARTSEASE.

" She hath done what she could." — MARK xiv. 8.

THERE is a good fable told about a king's garden, in which all at once the trees and flowers began to wither away: the oak, because it could not yield any fair flowers; the rose-bush, because it could bear no fruit; the vine, because it had to cling to the wall, and could cast no cool shad'ow.

" I am of no use in the world," said the oak.

" I might as well die," said the rose-bush.

" What good can I do ?" mur'mured the vine.

Then the king saw a little hearts'ease, which all this while held up its cheerful face, while all the rest were sad.

And the king said, " What makes you so bright and bloom-ing when all the rest are fading ? "

" I thought," said the little heartsease, " you wanted me here, because it was here you planted me; and so I thought I would try to be the best little heartsease that could be."

Little reader, are you like the oak, and the rose-bush, and the vine, doing nothing because you cannot do as much as others are doing ? Or will you be like the heartsease, and do your very best in the little corner of the vine'yard in which God's hand has put you?   T. S. HENDERSON.

MARCO.

I WILL tell you a true story of a bear who lived in a house by himself. He was a tame bear, and was called Marco. He was owned by a duke, whose name was Le'o-pold.

One cold night a poor little boy from Sa-voy was stray'ing about without any home or friends or food or warm clothes. Should you not have pit'ied him? Our Father in heaven pitied him, and took care of him in a strange way.

The poor boy came to Marco's hut; for he did not know that there was a bear in-side of it. The night, too, was dark, and the poor boy was cold and tired.

He lay down on the floor; and there he would have frozen most likely, if the tame bear had not come, and smelt of him, and then taken him in his fore-paws, and hugged him up to the warm fur of his breast. So the little boy went to sleep in the bear's em-brace, and slept warm all night.

He must have thought it quite odd the next day when he found himself held by a great black bear. But the bear gave him food to eat, and tend'ed him with as much care as if the little boy had been a little bear.

It is not often that the hug of a bear is so tender. I have known a bear to kill a man by hugging him to death. Per-haps Marco had been taught not to be so rough. If I ever meet a bear, I hope he will be a good and gentle bear like Marco; for then he will not hurt me.

When the duke heard that a little boy was in the bear's house, he came and saw for himself that the story was true. He led the little boy home, and gave him a nice suit of clothes, and took such care of him that the little boy did not suffer after that from want of food or of clothes.

175

THE RIDE.

PAUL means to take a short ride on his gay nag this fine June day.

His dog, Watch, will go with him, and run by the side of the nag.

They will go through the fields, where the cows graze, and by the side of the brook.

They will smell the new-mown grass, which the men toss with pitch-forks or rake into rows.

They will see the robins, that love so well to hop over the fresh rows, and search for food.

Paul loves to look at the trees and the grass and the flowers. He loves to hear the birds sing.

He has taught Watch that he must not chase the birds, or bark at them.

As soon as Paul comes home from his ride, he will get his books, and go straight to school.

He is a good boy; for he tries to do what is right, and to think what is right.

THE YOUNG HAIR-DRESSER.

S<small>EE</small> me brush my sister Ellen's hair. Ellen will sit still, and hold my doll, while I use the brush.

My name is Lucy, and I was four years old in May. I can

brush my own hair. I wear a net to hold it on the back of my head.

This is not my brush : it is my mother's. I have a small brush. I have a comb too, and I try to keep my hair neat and clean.

We have a dog, and his name is Jeff. He is a good dog, and does not bark at the horses that go by.

One day last week, Ellen and I were here in the room with no one by but Jeff. Mother had gone to market; and Jane, the maid, was in the yard, hanging out the clothes to dry.

All at once Jeff began to bark. We told him to hush; and, when he was still, we heard a heavy step on the stairs.

"Who can that be ?" said Ellen : "the front-door is locked. Who can have come into the house ? Is it a thief ?"

"Bow, wow, wow!" cried Jeff; and he put his fore-feet up against the door.

Then a gruff voice at the door said, "Let me in."

Jeff knew whose voice it was; for he wagged his tail, and stopped barking. But we did not know whose voice it was.

Ellen began to cry, but I did not cry.

"Let me in!" said the gruff voice once more. Then I knew it as well as Jeff did.

"Don't cry, Ellen," said I: "it is that naughty John, trying to scare us."

John is our brother. His school had been let out because the mistress was ill. He ran home, and climbed in at the window, and thought he would try to scare us.

Now, was he not a bad boy to try to scare us ? Mother told him if he ever did so again she should punish him. He has been a good boy since that; and, if his hair was not cut so short, I would like to brush it.

THE LITTLE BOY'S REBUKE.

THERE was once a very old man who lived in the house of his son. The old man was deaf; his eyes were dim, and his legs weak and thin. When he was at table he could hardly hold his spoon, so much did his hand shake; and at times he would spill his soup on the cloth.

All this vexed his son and the son's wife; and they made the old man sit in a corner behind the stove. There he ate his food from an earth'en-ware dish; and he had not always too much to eat, as you may guess.

Well, one day his trem'bling hands could not hold the dish: it fell on the floor, and broke. At this his son and his son's wife were so vexed that they spoke harsh'ly to the poor old man. His only an'swer was a deep, sad sigh. They then brought him a bowl made of wood, out of which he had to take his food.

Not long after this, his little grand'son, a boy of about four years of age, was seen at work with a chis'el and ham'mer, hol'low-ing out a log of wood.

His parents could not guess what he was trying to do. The little boy said nothing to any one, but kept at work on the log, and looked very grave, as if he had some great work in hand.

"What are you do'ing there?" asked his father. The little boy did not want to tell. Then his mother asked, "What are you do'ing, my son?"

"Oh!" said he, "I am only making a little trough, such as our pigs eat out of."

"But what are you making it for, my son?"

"I am making it," said he, "for you and father to eat out of when I am a man."

The parents looked at each other, and burst into tears.

From that time forth, they treated the old man well.   He had the best place at the table, a nice dish, and plenty of food.   Uncle Charles.

Pronounce *deaf*, dĕf ; *trough*, trŏf.   The *oo* in *spoon* is long.

————o○○○○——

SPRING VOICES.

"Caw! caw!" says the crow:
"Spring has come again, I know;
For, as sure as I am born,
There's a farm'er planting corn.
I shall break'fast there, I trow,
Long before his corn can grow."

"Quack! quack!" says the duck:
"Was there ever such good luck?
Spring has cleared this pond of ice;
And the day is warm and nice,
Just as I and Goodman Drake
Thought we'd like a swim to take."

"Croak! croak!" says the frog,
As he leaps out from the bog:
"The earth is warm and fair;
Spring is here, I do declare!
Croak! croak! I love the Spring;
Come, little birds, and sing."

KITTY CARELESS.

COME, come, Kitty Careless, the clock has struck nine !
Your hair still in papers ?   Is that quite the thing ?
   Can a bright girl like you
   Find nothing to do
But lounge in a bed-chamber, chewing a string ?

Just look at that work-box upset on the floor.
'Tis plain that your bureau is all in a mess ;
   Your apron's untied,
   And it's rumpled beside ;
Your shoulder is running away from your dress.

Jump up, little Kitty, and put things to rights:
Let's see how you look when your hair is in curl.
  I know, by your face,
  That your heart's in its place:
Now don't be, I pray, such a slat'tern-ly girl.

JANE OLIVER.

HOW THE CAT FED THE DOG.

Now I will tell you a true story of a cat and a dog.   The two were great friends.   They would jump and play for an hour at a time, and then they would lie down side by side.

The cat would put her paw on the dog's head, as much as to say, "If you sleep, I will take care of you."   So the cat would take care of the dog; and the dog would take care of the cat, for the dog would let no man or beast come near the cat to hurt her.

The dog's name was Wag.   If a big dog ran at the cat, to bite her or bark at her, Wag would rush at him, and make him run off much faster than he came.   Wag would let no one harm his dear friend the cat.

This cat had a queer name.   Her name was Tippet.   Now, one day, the dog and cat were left in a room; and on a shelf, high, high up, was a plate of good meat, cut in slices.

This meat the dog smelt out.   Then he looked and looked, till he spied out where the plate was.   But it was placed high up on the shelf; and how could he get at it?

Then he barked; and, by his bark, he must have told the cat that there was a nice plate of meat high up on the shelf, and that he would like to get at it if he could only climb like a cat.   And then Tippet said, "Mew!" which must have meant, "I will see what I can do for you, you dear old dog."

So the cat gave a leap; and up, up, high up on the top shelf she went, till she stood where she could reach the plate of meat. "Bow-wow!" said the dog, when he saw her there: by which he must have meant, "Oh, do throw me down a slice, dear Tippet!"

And, before she ate any herself, the cat took a slice, and threw it down to the dog; and the dog ate it, and then began to jump and bark for joy. And then, just as fast as the cat threw down the bits of meat, the dog would snap at them, and eat them up, and bark and bark for joy.

But it would have been wise in the dog not to bark so loud; for, when the cook heard him bark, she came to see why he barked so loud: and then she saw the cat sit on the shelf, and throw the meat to the dog; while the dog would snap at it, and eat it up as fast as it fell.

So the cook took a stick, and beat the dog; for he was a bad dog to eat the meat which was not his: and the dog did not bark for joy then, you may be sure; but he cried out in pain.

"And did not the cook beat Tippet, the cat, too?"

She did not beat her then; for Tippet was high up on the shelf, and the cook could not get at her: but I dare say the cat did not get off quite free; for she was a bad cat to steal the meat, though she did not eat it herself, but gave it to the dog.

"Was the dog much hurt by the beating he got?"

Not much; but he was hurt enough to make him remember that he must not steal meat.

TROTTIE'S AUNT.

OUT IN THE FIELDS.

Bring the children to the fields,
Where the sheep are straying;
With the birds and butterflies,
Let them now be playing;
On the hill-side, in the glen,
All the green lawn over,
Through the yellow buttercups,
Down among the clover!

With the sunshine in their hearts,
In their cheeks the roses,
Let them breathe the balmy air,
Let them gather posies.
In this merry month of June,
Summer's fairest weather,
Let the children and the flowers
Bud and bloom together.　　　ANNA LIVINGSTON.

184

LOOK UP.

Two little boys once went to sea with their uncle to learn to be sail'ors. One day he said to them, "Come, my boys, you will never learn to be sailors if you don't learn to climb; let me see if you can follow me up the mast."

So the uncle went high up on the mast, and the boys began to climb up after him. But one of them had not climbed far, when he looked round, and, seeing how high up he was, began to get diz'zy and fright'ened, and cried out, "O uncle! I shall fall; I am sure I shall fall; what am I to do?"

"Look up, look up, my boy!" said his uncle: "if you look down, you will be gid'dy; but, if you keep look'ing up to the flag at the top of the mast, you may mount or go down safe'ly."

The boy took his uncle's advice, and then found that he could go up and down the mast without being diz'zy. Both the little boys soon became good sailors.

Now, what should we do when we sink in grief or fear? Why, we should look up,—up to the heaven above us; fix our thought on Him who is the Father of all, and from whom all strength must come. Trusting in Him, we need not fear; since, whether we live or die, His tender mercies are over all his works.

THE CHILDREN AND THE SPARROW.

CHILDREN.

" You dear little bird, you brisk little bird,
　　What charming songs you sing !
Come down from the tree, and play with us :
　　We love you, you pretty thing."

SPARROW.

" Indeed, my dear childen, it will not do ;
　　You see I must earn my bread :
I've five little hungry birds in my nest,
　　And all of them must be fed."

THE LITTLE BROWN THING.

I know a little girl whose name is Annie. One day in the garden, she stopped to smell of a red rose ; and, while she was stooping down to smell of it, she saw a queer little brown thing hanging under a leaf.

"Why, what can this little brown thing be?" said Annie to herself. "It looks like a shell. I do wonder what it is! I must find out what it is."

So she took a stick, and touched it softly; but it did not move. Then she touched it again with more force, and it fell from the leaf on to the ground. It did not seem to be alive; and yet she did not like to touch it with her fingers.

She put her face close down to it,—so close, that she almost fell over; but she could not tell what it was. So she ran to her mother; and her mother came out, and took up the little brown thing, and put it on a leaf.

Then, taking it into the house, she put it under a tum'bler, on a table by the window, and told Annie not to touch it. Annie was very curious to pick it to pieces, and see what was inside of it; but she told her mother she would not touch it, and she kept her word.

"I think," said her mother, "you will not have to wait longer than ten days before you will see this little brown thing open of itself, and show you what is inside of it."

Annie thought this very strange. Day after day she would come and look at the little brown thing, as it lay there quite still under the tumbler; and at last she saw it move. She called her mother, and the two watched the little thing till out of it came a butterfly like the one of which I give you a picture on the next page.

Then Annie's mother told her that this butterfly was once a cat'er-pil-lar. At first it was no bigger than the head of a small pin. Then it grew, and began to eat the green leaves. It had eyes, and could see; and many feet, and could crawl; but it had no wings.

By and by it passed into a state in which it was folded in a shroud, or cover, where it did not move, and did not eat. It was in this state when Annie found it; and now let me tell you that the insect, when in this state, is called a *chrys'-a-lis.**

And from this shroud the bright, beautiful butterfly came forth at last to sport in the sun, and please us with the rich hues of its wings. These hues seem to the eye like a fine dust; but, if you will look at them through the right sort of glass, you will see that they are thin feather-like scales, one lapping over the other like the scales of a fish.

After Annie had admired the butterfly, her mother said to

her, " I hope you will not forget what you have learnt to-day. When you see a caterpillar, do not be sorry that it is ugly, and crawls on the ground, and has no wings; but say to yourself, ' This caterpillar will be a beautiful butterfly by and by.' "

* It is so called because of the golden color of certain species. The Greek word *chrusos* means *gold.*

WILLIAM'S ROSE-BUSH.

HERE is a picture of the rose which William plucked last week from his own bush, and gave to his mother.

June is sometimes called "the month of roses;" for there are more beautiful roses in bloom out of doors this month than at any other time during the year.

I will tell you how William came to own a rose-bush. A year ago last May, as he was passing by a greenhouse where flowers were kept, he saw a man empty a cart of rub'bish by the side of the road.

In the rubbish, among other vines, William saw a small rose-bush. So he went up to the man, and said, "Did you mean to throw away this rose-bush?"

"Yes," said the man: "we will thank you for taking away all you may find in this heap."

"Then I will take this rose-bush," said William; "for I do not think it is dead."

" You are quite welcome to it," said the man.

So William took it home, and set it out in his little garden. How glad he was when he found that the bush was a-live, and that the leaf-buds had be-gun to start!

He took great care of his rose-bush. He kept it free from weeds. He kept the soil loose around it. When the weather was dry, he gave it water; and, when the frost came, he tied up the branches with straw, so that they might not be hurt by the cold.

The bush bore no roses the first spring; but this year it has borne those you see in the picture, and more besides. How proud William was to take them to his mother! He knows she is fond of roses.

He thinks that next week there will be three more roses in bloom on his bush; and these he means to take to his teacher. How pleas'ant it is, if we can give nothing of great val'ue, to give at least flow'ers to those we love, — to those who try to serve us!

William loves his rose-bush for many reasons: first, because flowers are the gift of the good God, who creates things of beauty as well as things of use; but William also loves his rose-bush be-cause he can make others happy by giving them the roses.

MORNING HYMN.

THE night is gone, the morning breaks;
Upon the bank the flower awakes;
And, when the sun is on his way,
The woods look golden in his ray.

Each blade of grass has beads of dew;
The sky is cloudless, soft, and blue ;
The little birds, on every side,
Are singing of the sweet spring-tide.

Nor shall they sing alone, while I
Have life beneath the sunny sky;
While I can thank the God who made
Sun, sky, sweet birds, and dewy blade.

ALBERT VICTOR.

SOME of our young friends may live to see the little boy, whose likeness we here give, king of England. His name is Albert Victor. He is a son of the Prince of Wales, and grandson of Victoria, now Queen of England. He was born the 9th of January, 1864. Can you reckon how old he is at this time ?

If we may judge from his picture, he is a bright-looking little fellow; and we hope he will grow up to be a good and wise man. We are doing all we can to make him one; for we send him "The Nursery" every month. If he will learn to read it as well as some little American boys, not older than he, can read it, he will find it a great help to him as well as a great pleasure.

In this country, we have no kings to rule us, and we do not want any; for here we think that the people ought to choose their chief as often as once every four years. Such a choice a people can safely make, if they will all learn to read and write, and if they will love and strive after the good and the true.   But if they will not learn, or try to be good, then the country will be in danger; then we may have kings to rule us.

So let every American child — let all our boys and girls — bear in mind that they ought to learn to read and write. For their country's sake, they ought to do this.   They ought

ALBERT VICTOR, Born Jan. 9, 1864.

to learn much about their own great country, and feel a wish to do good to all men in all parts of the world.

As Prince Albert will have "The Nursery" to help him, we hope that all the little boys and girls in the United States will have it too, so that they may learn to read quite as well as he; and then should he grow up to be a good, wise king, and should you grow up to be a good, wise man or woman, you can say, "We both used to read out of the same little book when we were children."